Samuel Johnson

A Memoir of Roger Ascham

With an Introduction by James H Carlisle

Samuel Johnson

A Memoir of Roger Ascham
With an Introduction by James H. Carlisle

ISBN/EAN: 9783744721066

Printed in Europe, USA, Canada, Australia, Japan

Cover: Foto ©Raphael Reischuk / pixelio.de

More available books at **www.hansebooks.com**

CHAUTAUQUA LIBRARY.....GARNET SERIES.

A MEMOIR

OF

ROGER ASCHAM.

BY

SAMUEL JOHNSON, LL. D.

(ORIGINALLY PUBLISHED IN LONDON IN 1763.)

WITH AN INTRODUCTION

BY

JAMES H. CARLISLE,

PRESIDENT OF WOFFORD COLLEGE, SPARTANBURG, S.C.

BOSTON:

CHAUTAUQUA PRESS,

117 FRANKLIN STREET.

1886.

ROGER ASCHAM

(1515–1568)

AND

THOMAS ARNOLD

(1795–1842)

CONTENTS.

INTRODUCTION.

ROGER ASCHAM (As'-kam) has a claim on all English-reading people. He is called, by the best critics, one of the fathers of English prose. In his youth, his native language had no great work in poetry, history, or philosophy. The wonderful art of printing was in its infancy. His father may have read the first book printed in England when fresh from the press. Soon after Ascham, a constellation of great writers adorned the latter years of Elizabeth's reign. At his death, Shakspeare was four years old, Bacon seven, Sidney fourteen, and Spenser sixteen.

His first work, "TOXOPHILUS," published in his twenty-third year, was a defence of the bow, which he looked upon as furnishing a manly recreation, as well as a national defence, to Englishmen. The year of publication, 1544, was the date when pistols were first used by English horsemen. The musket was first used a few years before, 1521. Ascham could not know that these strange weapons would soon come to be considered as the strong "arms" of English soldiers. Three years after "Toxophilus" appeared, bows were used with effect, for the last time, on the field of Pinkie, where the Scotch were forced to give way before the arrows of their invaders. As a pleasant recreation, Archery, at intervals, comes into fashion for a time, as it did with us a few years ago. The lovers of archery show their gratitude to Ascham by giving his name to the closet in which their weapons are kept.

But the work on the Bow has a permanent value in our history. It marks an era in the growth of our language. He dedicated it to his king, Henry VIII., apologizing for writing in English, and offering to prepare a Greek or Latin version if desired. He says, "To have written in another tongue had been more profitable for my study, and more honest [honorable] for my name; yet I can think my labour well bestowed, if, with a little hindrance of my profit and name, may come any furtherance to the pleasure or commodity of the *gentlemen and yeomen of England.* As for the Latin or Greek tongue, every thing is so excellently done in them, that none can do better; in the English tongue, contrary, *every thing in a manner so meanly both for the matter and handling, that no man can do worse.*"

This little book, on two occasions, turned the current of the author's life. Henry was graciously pleased to reward him on its first appearance; and a few years later, Edward renewed his pension for its sake. His "Report and Discourse of the Affairs of Germany" is the only other work published in his lifetime.

Ascham has an additional claim on all who are interested in educational literature. He is the first who wrote in our language on such subjects. He left, in manuscript, an unfinished work, "T.HE SCHOLEMASTER," which was published by his widow in 1570. Extracts from this book, and the "Preface to the Reader," will be given in another chapter. It has had a rather singular history. Within twenty years of the author's death, five editions were issued. For more than a century it was then strangely overlooked. In 1711 Rev. James Upton published an edition of "The Scholemaster," with explanatory notes. Again, in 1743, Upton issued another edition, "revised a second time, and much improved." In 1763 the "English Works of Roger Ascham" were published in London by James Bennet as editor. For this edition, Dr. Samuel Johnson wrote a memoir of the author. This is so good a specimen of the great Doctor's peculiar style, and is so instructive every way, that it is now republished entire.

There is something to interest the general reader in this brief record of a life, which had connection, more or less intimate, with four successive English sovereigns, — Henry VIII., Edward VI, Mary, and Elizabeth. Under the last three, he held the post of Latin secretary, an honorable office, like that which Milton held under Cromwell a century later. While doing much to give beauty and force to his own language, he was a passionate lover of Latin and Greek. Dr. Johnson bears testimony to Ascham's skill in the

manual art of writing.   His successors in the "schole-
room" should avoid the two opposite mistakes that
may be easily made in this matter.   To be a "good
scribe" is not the only qualification needed in a teacher.
Yet to write legibly is not so trifling an accomplish-
ment that it may be neglected.   Do not schools and
colleges in our day dismiss many pupils untaught in
this elementary part of a common education?

Very much of the scholarship of that day consisted
in the study of Latin, and especially of Greek, then
becoming fashionable in literary circles.   It is difficult
for us to conceive the interest with which scholars
then discussed the question of admitting this new
study, and the true pronunciation of the alphabet.
Wade, in his "British History," says, "Many, both of
the secular and regular clergy, railed against the Greek
Testament of Erasmus as an impious and dangerous
book.   At Oxford they were divided into factions, —
one assuming the name of Greeks, the other of
Trojans.   As the Trojans were the most numerous,
they were the most insolent.   When a poor Greek
appeared in the street in any public place, he was
attacked by the Trojans with hisses, taunts, and insults
of all kinds.   But the triumphs of the Trojans were
of short duration.   Henry VIII. and Wolsey having
warmly espoused the cause of the Greeks, their numbers, their credit, and their courage daily increased:
the Greek language became a favorite study, and the
Trojans were obliged to retire from the field."   Ascham
left no original work in Greek or Latin, not even a

new edition of a favorite classical author. Still, he was an enthusiastic reader and teacher of the classics all through life. He was the tutor of Elizabeth in her early years, when she scarcely expected to reach the throne. After her accession it was very honorable to both parties that she invited her old teacher to come and still direct her studies. He read with her most of the works of Cicero, the greater portion of Livy, select portions of Isocrates, the Tragedies of Sophocles, the Greek Testament, and other works. She wrote several volumes, which show her skill as a linguist. When she visited Oxford, she readily replied in Latin to a learned address of welcome. Her teacher says, " I learn more from her than she from me : I teach her words, while she teaches me things." It is probable that some of the milder traits that throw a redeeming light on the strong character of the imperious Virgin Queen were due to the influence of her teacher.

As to his manner of teaching, we know nothing, except as he has explained it in his treatise. With his scholarship and enthusiasm, and with such pupils as he usually had, he could do good work, with any plan, or in the absence of a plan. The transition from a teacher in the sixteenth century, with a few noble pupils, to the teacher in the nineteenth century, ruling forty little "sovereigns" in this New World, is very great. Yet there are lessons in Ascham's life for us. He was happy in his work. When absent in Germany, he looked back longingly to his work at home. His views on discipline were far in advance of his

time. His genial, sympathetic spirit furnishes some
good lessons to the teachers of to-day. He received
only a moderate salary, and doubtless he had to prac-
tise economy, not an easy thing in a court. He was
unselfish. If extravagant, it was not in dress, or style
of living, but in buying books. He once offered to
commute a part of his "fees" for an old classical
book. "He was ready to assist students with advice,
and generous to poor scholars," said a contemporary.
This short sentence may open a wide door of usefulness to the teacher with a scanty income. Sympathy
and kindness may do much good with little money.
The old teacher was not above the professional weakness of boasting about his distinguished pupils. Let
the American schoolmaster who can keep his republi-
can humility when several pupils have reached titles
and crowns, prepare to cast a stone ! He was grateful to his old teachers. He often refers kindly to his
illustrious "master, John Cheke." About another of
his teachers he says something worth quoting for the
reader : "Doctor Nico Medcalfe, that honourable father,
was Master of S. John's College when I came thither ;
a man meanly learned himself, but not meanly affec-
tioned to set forward learning in others. . . . Truly
he was partial to none, but impartial to all ; a master
for the whole, a father to every one in that College.
There was none so poor, if he had either will in goodness, or wit to learning, that could lacke being there,
or should depart from thence for any need. I am witness myself, that money many times was brought into

young men's studies by strangers whom they knew not.
. . . I myself, one of the meanest of a great number
in that College, because there appeared in me some
small show of towardness and diligence, lacked not
his favour to further me in learning." And thus, a
man, himself "meanly furnished with knowledge,"
may kindle the torch of a young Ascham : the stream
of learning may rise above its source. This is an in-
spiring thought to the earnest teacher.

As a man, there is much in him to excite our interest, and even our admiration. The reigns of his four
monarchs span an eventful period of history. The
faithful teacher passed through it, in the main, un-
tainted. He knew how to close eyes and ears when
necessary. He served his pupil and his queen, holding this double, delicate relation, and meeting all its
most exacting demands. He did not beg or fawn. He
was grateful, but not obsequious, to patrons. He respected alike himself and his sovereign. We may
regret that an excessive caution, or indolence, hindered
his pen from doing all the service it was so able to
render. His diary, kept through these critical years,
would now be a great treasure to the lover of minute
history, and to the student of human nature. No
gossip or intrigue is associated with the memory of
Elizabeth's teacher. The public history of her reign
could be written without alluding to his name, perhaps.
It is true, unfortunately, that he did not move the
Queen to any great liberality towards schools or scholars. She endowed Dublin University and Westminster

School. Her long reign shows no other benefaction to institutions of learning. But Ascham did not advance his own interests by her affection for him. The associate of nobles and monarchs all through his public life, he died poor, leaving his children no legacy but his fame, and the unfinished manuscript of "The Scholemaster." Dr. Johnson very delicately alludes to his love of gaming. It is quite probable, that, in this matter, he did not rise above the customs of the day. A contemporary historian, after describing the baiting of bulls and bears, adds, "To this entertainment, there follows that of whipping a blinded bear, which is performed by five or six men, standing circularly with whips, which they exercise on him without mercy, as he cannot escape from them, because of his chain. He defends himself with all his force and skill, throwing them down that come within his reach, and not active enough to get out of it, and tearing their whips out of their hands, and breaking them." The Queen encouraged such sports. Here is the programme for a few days, from the "Sidney Papers:" "This day she appoints a Frenchman to doe feats upon a rope in the conduit-yard; to-morrow, she has commanded the bears, the bulls, and the apes to be bayted in the tilt-yard; and, on Wednesday, she will have solemne dauncing." Among the offices she conferred on her favorite teacher, was that of her "bear-keeper," — not altogether a sinecure, it is to be feared. In such an age, we cannot imagine that all the dice-throwing and card-playing were "just for fun." Manners and morals were at a low ebb in some respects. Let us try to imagine a "bear-baiting in the tilt-yard" of Windsor Palace, honored by the presence of the noble woman who to-day sits on Elizabeth's throne. We readily see that the three centuries between the two queens have witnessed some changes. Vinet says, "'The conscience of humanity never restores any of its conquests." The friends of "humanity" should neither despond, nor be very sanguine.

While throwing the veil of charity over the recreations of the courtly schoolmaster, we may be interested or amused at the coloring which they occasionally give to his style. Thus, in the posthumous treatise, he says, "I dare venture a good wager," etc. Again, "I have been a looker-on in the cock-pit of learning these many years." Let us, however, follow the advice of Dr. Johnson, and think of the learning, virtues, and excellences of Ascham, rather than of the frailties of his age, which he shared. Even his gaming does not seem to have familiarized him with debts or dishonor. In an age of persecution and bloodshed, there is no stain on his memory. At a time of religious bigotry, he kept his consistency and the respect of all parties to an unusual degree. He was a lover of peace, good men, and good books. As far as can be known, his language and his life were pure. Such outward tests of a religious character as can be applied, place him in a favorable light. "His conversation had a strain of unaffected piety in it, and he was regular in his private devotions. The topics of discussion among his friends were of God; the iniquity and malice of mankind; the effects of God's benevolence towards them; the grand designs of Providence, to lead men to their greatest and ultimate happiness." Such is the testimony of one who knew him well. He died in his fifty-third year, — about the age to which Shakspeare attained. Elizabeth gave a characteristic proof of her regret, by saying, "I would rather have thrown ten thousand pounds into the sea, than lose my Ascham." His learned contemporary, George Buchanan of Scotland, wrote an "Epigram," which may stand as a just estimate of the man.

> "Aschamum extinctum patriæ Graiæ Camenæ
> Et Latinæ vera cum pietate dolent.
> Principibus vixit carus, jucundus amicis,
> Re modica; in mores dicere fama nequit."

It has been freely translated thus : —

> "His country's Muses join with those of Greece
> And mighty Rome to mourn the fate of Ascham.
> Dear to his Prince, and valued by his friends,
> Content with humble views, thro' life he passed;
> While envy's self ne'er dared to blast his name."

JAS. H. CARLISLE.

SPARTANBURG, S.C., April 13, 1886.

ROGER ASCHAM.

By SAMUEL JOHNSON, LL.D.

CHAPTER I.

IT often happens to writers, that they are known only by their works; the incidents of a literary life are seldom observed, and therefore seldom recounted: but Ascham has escaped the common fate by the friendship of Edward Graunt, the learned master of Westminster school, who devoted an oration to his memory, and has marked the various vicissitudes of his fortune. Graunt either avoided the labor of minute inquiry, or thought domestic occurrences unworthy of his notice; or, preferring the character of an orator to that of an historian, selected only such particulars as he could best express or most happily embellish. His narrative is therefore scanty, and I know not by what materials it can now be amplified.

ROGER ASCHAM was born in the year 1515, at Kirby Wiske (or Kirby Wicke), a village near Northallerton, in Yorkshire, of a family above the vulgar. His father,

John Ascham, was house-steward in the family of Scroop, and in that age, when the different orders of men were at a greater distance from each other, and the manners of gentlemen were regularly formed by menial services in great houses, lived with a very conspicuous reputation. Margaret Ascham, his wife, is said to be allied to many considerable families; but her maiden name is not recorded. She had three sons, of whom Roger was the youngest, and some daughters; but who can hope, that, of any progeny, more than one shall deserve to be mentioned? They lived married sixty-seven [1] years, and at last died together, almost on the same hour of the same day.

Roger, having passed his first years under the care of his parents, was adopted into the family of Antony Wingfield, who maintained him, and committed his education, with that of his own sons, to the care of one Bond, a domestic tutor. He very early discovered an unusual fondness for literature by an eager perusal of English books, and, having passed happily through the scholastic rudiments, was put, in 1530, by his patron, Wingfield, to St. John's College, in Cambridge.

Ascham entered Cambridge at a time when the last great revolution of the intellectual world was filling every academical mind with ardor or anxiety. The destruction of the Constantinopolitan empire had driven the Greeks with their language into the interior parts of Europe. The art of printing had made the books easily attainable, and the Greek now began to

---

[1] Other authorities say *forty-seven.* — C.

be taught in England. The doctrines of Luther had already filled all the nations of the Romish communion with controversy and dissension. New studies of literature, and new tenets of religion, found employment for all who were desirous of truth, or ambitious of fame. Learning was at that time prosecuted with that eagerness and perseverance which in this age of indifference and dissipation it is not easy to conceive. To teach or to learn, was at once the business and the pleasure of the academical life; and an emulation of study was raised by Cheke and Smith, to which even the present age, perhaps, owes many advantages, without remembering or knowing its benefactors.

Ascham soon resolved to unite himself to those who were enlarging the bounds of knowledge, and, immediately upon his admission into the college, applied himself to the study of Greek. Those who were zealous for the new learning, were often no great friends to the old religion; and Ascham, as he became a Grecian, became a Protestant. The Reformation was not yet begun: disaffection to Popery was considered as a crime justly punished by exclusion from favor and preferment, and was not yet openly professed, though superstition was gradually losing its hold upon the public. The study of Greek was reputable enough, and Ascham pursued it with diligence and success equally conspicuous. He thought a language might be most easily learned by teaching it, and, when he had obtained some proficiency in Greek, read lectures, while he was yet a boy, to other boys, who were desir-

ous of instruction. His industry was much encouraged
by Pember, a man of great eminence at that time;
though I know not that he has left any monuments
behind him, but what the gratitude of his friends and
scholars has bestowed. He was one of the great en-
couragers of Greek learning, and particularly applaud-
ed Ascham's lectures, assuring him, in a letter, of
which Graunt has preserved an extract, that he would
gain more knowledge by explaining one of Æsop's
fables to a boy, than by hearing one of Homer's poems
explained by another.

Ascham took his bachelor's degree in 1534 (Feb.
18), in the eighteenth year of his age, — a time of life
at which it is more common now to enter the universities than to take degrees, but which, according to the
modes of education then in use, had nothing of remarkable prematurity. On the 23d of March following, he was chosen fellow of the college, which election
he considered as a second birth. Dr. Metcalf, the
master of the college, a man, as Ascham tells us,
"meanly learned himself, but no mean encourager of
learning in others," clandestinely promoted his election, though he openly seemed first to oppose it, and
afterwards to censure it, because Ascham was known
to favor the new opinions; and the master himself
was accused of giving an unjust preference to the
Northern men, one of the factions into which this
nation was divided, before we could find any more
important reason of dissension, than that some were
born on the northern and some on the southern side

of Trent. Any cause is sufficient for a quarrel; and the zealots of the north and south lived long in such animosity, that it was thought necessary at Oxford to keep them quiet by choosing one proctor every year from each.

He seems to have been hitherto supported by the bounty of Wingfield, which his attainment of a fellowship now freed him from the necessity of receiving. Dependence, though in those days it was more common, and less irksome, than in the present state of things, can never have been free from discontent; and therefore he that was released from it must always have rejoiced. The danger is, lest the joy of escaping from the patron may not leave sufficient memory of the benefactor. Of this forgetfulness, Ascham cannot be accused; for he is recorded to have preserved the most grateful and affectionate reverence for Wingfield, and to have never grown weary of recounting his benefits.

His reputation still increased, and many resorted to his chamber to hear the Greek writers explained. He was likewise eminent for other accomplishments. By the advice of Pember, he had learned to play on musical instruments; and he was one of the few who excelled in the mechanical art of writing, which then began to be cultivated among us, and in which we now surpass all other nations. He not only wrote his pages with neatness, but embellished them with elegant draughts and illuminations, — an art at that time so highly valued, that it contributed much, both to his fame and his fortune.

He became Master of Arts in March, 1537, in his twenty-first year, and then, if not before, commenced tutor, and publicly undertook the education of young men. A tutor of one and twenty, however accomplished with learning, however exalted by genius, would now gain little reverence or obedience; but in those days of discipline and regularity, the authority of the statutes easily supplied that of the teacher; all power that was lawful was reverenced. Besides, young tutors had still younger pupils.

Ascham is said to have courted his scholars to study by every incitement, to have treated them with great kindness, and to have taken care at once to instil learning and piety, to enlighten their minds, and to form their manners. Many of his scholars rose to great eminence; and among them William Grindal was so much distinguished, that, by Cheke's recommendation, he was called to court as a proper master of languages for the Lady Elizabeth.

There was yet no established lecturer of Greek: the university therefore appointed Ascham to read in the open schools, and paid him out of the public purse an honorary stipend, such as was then reckoned sufficiently liberal. A lecture was afterwards founded by King Henry; and he then quitted the schools, but continued to explain Greek authors in his own college.

He was at first an opponent of the new pronunciation introduced, or rather of the ancient restored, about this time by Cheke and Smith, and made some cautious struggles for the common practice, which the credit and dignity of his antagonists did not permit him to defend very publicly, or with much vehemence : nor were they long his antagonists ; for either his affection for their merit, or his conviction of the cogency of their arguments, soon changed his opinion and his practice, and he adhered ever after to their method of utterance.

Of this controversy it is not necessary to give a circumstantial account ; something of it may be found in Strype's "Life of Smith," and something in Baker's "Reflections upon Learning : " it is sufficient to remark here, that Cheke's pronunciation was that which now prevails in the schools of England. Disquisitions not only verbal, but merely literal, are too minute for popular narration.

He was not less eminent as a writer of Latin, than as a teacher of Greek. All the public letters of the university were of his composition ; and as little qualifications must often bring great abilities into notice, he was recommended to this honorable employment, not less by the neatness of his hand, than the elegance of his style.

However great was his learning, he was not always immured in his chamber, but being valetudinary, and weak of body, thought it necessary to spend many hours in such exercises as might best relieve him after the fatigue of study. His favorite amusement was archery, in which he spent, or, in the opinion of others, lost, so much time, that those whom either his faults or virtues made his enemies, and perhaps some whose kindness wished him always worthily employed, did not scruple to censure his practice, as unsuitable to a man professing learning, and perhaps of bad example in a place of education.

To free himself from this censure was one of the reasons for which he published, in 1544, his "Toxophilus, or the Schole or Partitions of Shooting," in which he joins the praise with the precepts of archery. He designed not only to teach the art of shooting, but to give an example of diction more natural and more truly English than was used by the common writers of that age, whom he censures for mingling exotic terms with their native language, and of whom he complains that they were made authors, not by skill or education, but by arrogance and temerity.

He has not failed in either of his purposes. He has sufficiently vindicated archery as an innocent, salutary, useful, and liberal diversion ; and if his precepts are of no great use, he has only shown, by one example among many, how little the hand can derive from the mind, how little intelligence can conduce to dexterity. In every art, practice is much : in arts manual, practice is almost the whole. Precept can at most but warn against error : it can never bestow excellence.

The bow has been so long disused, that most English readers have forgotten its importance, though it was the weapon by which we gained the battle of Agincourt, — a weapon which, when handled by English yeomen, no foreign troops were able to resist. We were not only abler of body than the French, and therefore superior in the use of arms, which are forcible only in proportion to the strength with which they are handled, but the national practice of shooting for pleasure or for prizes, by which every man was inured to archery from his infancy, gave us insuperable advantage, the bow requiring more practice to skilful use than any other instrument of offence.

Fire-arms were then in their infancy; and though battering-pieces had been some time in use, I know not whether any soldiers were armed with hand-guns when the "Toxophilus" was first published. They were soon after used by the Spanish troops, whom other nations made haste to imitate; but how little they could yet effect will be understood from the account given by the ingenious author of the "Exercise for the Norfolk Militia."

"The first muskets were very heavy, and could not be fired without a rest: they had matchlocks, and barrels of a wide bore, that carried a large ball and charge of powder, and did execution at a greater distance.

"The musketeers on a march carried only their rests and ammunition, and had boys to bear their muskets after them, for which they were allowed great additional pay.

"They were very slow in loading, not only by reason of the unwieldiness of the pieces, and because they carried the powder and balls separate, but from the time it took to prepare and adjust the match; so that their fire was not near so brisk as ours is now. Afterwards a lighter kind of matchlock musket came into use: and they carried their ammunition in bandeliers, which were broad belts that came over the shoulder, to which were hung several little cases of wood covered with leather, each containing a charge of powder; the balls they carried loose in a pouch; and they had also a priming-horn hanging by their side.   .

"The old English writers call those large muskets calivers: the harquebuze was a lighter piece, that could be fired without a rest. The matchlock was fired by a match fixed by a kind of tongs in the serpentine, or cock, which, by pulling the trigger, was brought down with great quickness upon the priming in the pan, over which there was a sliding cover, which was drawn back by the hand just at the time of firing. There was a great deal of nicety and care required to fit the match properly to the cock, so as to come down exactly true on the priming, to blow the ashes from the coal, and to guard the pan from the sparks that fell from it. A great deal of time was also lost in taking it out of the cock, and returning it between the fingers of the left hand every time that the piece was fired; and wet weather often rendered the matches useless."

While this was the state of fire-arms, — and this state continued among us to the civil war with very little improvement, — it is no wonder that the long-bow was preferred by Sir Thomas Smith, who wrote of the choice of weapons in the reign of Queen Elizabeth, when the use of the bow still continued, though the musket was gradually prevailing. Sir John Hayward, a writer yet later, has, in his history of the Norman kings, endeavored to evince the superiority of the archer to the musketeer: however, in the long peace of King James, the bow was wholly forgotten. Guns have from that time been the weapons of the English, as of other nations, and, as they are now improved, are certainly more efficacious.

Ascham had yet another reason, if not for writing his book, at least for presenting it to King Henry.

England was not then what it may be now justly termed, the capital of literature ; and therefore, those who aspired to superior degrees of excellence thought it necessary to travel into other countries. The purse of Ascham was not equal to the expense of peregrination, and therefore he hoped to have it augmented by a pension. Nor was he wholly disappointed, for the king rewarded him with a yearly payment of ten pounds.

A pension of ten pounds, granted by a king of England to a man of letters, appears to modern readers so contemptible a benefaction, that it is not unworthy of inquiry what might be its value at that time, and how much Ascham might be enriched by it. Nothing is more uncertain than the estimation of wealth by denominated money ; the precious metals never retain long the same proportion to real commodities, and the same names in different ages do not imply the same quantity of metal ; so that it is equally difficult to know how much money was contained in any nominal sum, and to find what any supposed quantity of gold or silver would purchase, both which are necessary to the commensuration of money, or the adjustment of proportion between the same sums at different periods of time.

A numeral pound in King Henry's time contained, as now, twenty shillings ; and therefore it must be inquired what twenty shillings could perform. Breadcorn is the most certain standard of the necessaries of life. Wheat was generally sold at that time for one shilling the bushel : if, therefore, we take five shillings

the bushel for the current price, ten pounds were
equivalent to fifty. But here is danger of a fallacy.
It may be doubted whether wheat was the general
bread-corn of that age; and if rye, barley, or oats
were the common food, and wheat, as I suspect, only
a delicacy, the value of wheat will not regulate the
price of other things. This doubt, however, is in favor
of Ascham; for, if we raise the worth of wheat, we
raise that of his pension.

But the value of money has another variation, which
we are still less able to ascertain : the rules of custom,
or the different needs of artificial life, make that reve-
nue little at one time which is great at another. Men
are rich and poor, not only in proportion to what they
have, but to what they want. In some ages, not only
necessaries are cheaper, but fewer things are necessary.
In the age of Ascham, most of the elegances and ex-
penses of our present fashions were unknown; com-
merce had not yet distributed superfluity through the
lower classes of the people; and the character of a
student implied frugality, and required no splendor to
support it. His pension, therefore, reckoning together
the wants which he could supply, and the wants from
which he was exempt, may be estimated, in my opinion, at more than a hundred pounds a year, which,
added to the income of his fellowship, put him far
enough above distress.

This was a year of good fortune to Ascham. He
was chosen orator to the university on the removal of
Sir John Cheke to court, where he was made tutor

to Prince Edward. A man once distinguished soon gains admirers. Ascham was now received to notice by many of the nobility, and by great ladies, among whom it was then the fashion to study the ancient languages. Lee, archbishop of York, allowed him a yearly pension : how much, we are not told. He was probably about this time employed in teaching many illustrious persons to write a fine hand, and among others, Henry and Charles, dukes of Suffolk, the Princess Elizabeth, and Prince Edward.

Henry VIII. died two years after ; and a reformation of religion being now openly prosecuted by King Edward and his council, Ascham, who was known to favor it, had a new grant of his pension, and continued at Cambridge, where he lived in great familiarity with Bucer, who had been called from Germany to the professorship of divinity. But his retirement was soon at an end ; for in 1548, his pupil Grindal, the master of the Princess Elizabeth, died ; and the princess, who had already some acquaintance with Ascham, called him from his college to direct her studies. He obeyed the summons, as we may easily believe, with readiness, and for two years instructed her with great diligence ; but then, being disgusted either at her or her domestics, perhaps eager for another change of life, he left her without her consent, and returned to the university. Of this precipitation he long repented ; and, as those who are not accustomed to disrespect cannot easily forgive it, he probably felt the effects of his imprudence to his death.

After having visited Cambridge, he took a journey into Yorkshire, to see his native place and his old acquaintance, and there received a letter from the court, informing him that he was appointed secretary to Sir Richard Morisine, who was to be despatched as ambassador into Germany. In his return to London, he paid that memorable visit to Lady Jane Grey, in which he found her reading the " Phædo," in Greek, as he has related in his " Schole Master."

In September, 1550, he attended Morisine to Germany, and wandered over great part of the country, making observations upon all that appeared worthy of his curiosity, and contracting acquaintance with men of learning. To his correspondent Sturmius he paid a visit; but Sturmius was not at home, and those two illustrious friends never saw each other. During the course of this embassy, Ascham undertook to improve Morisine in Greek, and, for four days in the week, explained some passages in Herodotus every morning, and more than two hundred verses of Sophocles or Euripides every afternoon. He read with him likewise some of the orations of Demosthenes. On the other days he compiled the letters of business, and in the night filled up his diary, digested his remarks, and wrote private letters to his friends in England, and particularly to those of his college, whom he continually exhorted to perseverance in study. Amidst all the pleasures of novelty which his travels supplied, and in the dignity of his public station, he preferred the tranquillity of private study and the quiet of academical retirement. The reasonableness of this choice has been always disputed ; and in the contrariety of human interests and dispositions, the controversy will not easily be decided. ·

He made a short excursion into Italy, and mentions in his "Schole Master," with great severity, the vices of Venice. He was desirous of visiting Trent while the council were sitting, but the scantiness of his purse defeated his curiosity.

In this journey he wrote his " Report and Discourse of the Affairs in Germany," in which he describes the dispositions and interests of the German princes like a man inquisitive and judicious, and recounts many particularities which are lost in the mass of general history, in a style which to the ears of that age was undoubtedly mellifluous, and which is now a very valuable specimen of genuine English.

By the death of King Edward in 1553, the Reformation was stopped, Morisine was recalled, and Ascham's pension and hopes were at an end. He therefore retired to his fellowship in a state of disappointment and despair, which his biographer has endeavored to express in the deepest strain of plaintive declamation. "He was deprived of all his support," says Graunt, "stripped of his pension, and cut off from the assistance of his friends, who had now lost their influence ; so that he had *nec præmia nec prædia,* neither pension nor estate to support him at Cambridge." There is no credit due to a rhetorician's account, either of good or evil. The truth is, that Ascham still had in his

fellowship all that in the early part of his life had given
him plenty, and might have lived like the other inhabitants of the college, with the advantage of more
knowledge and higher reputation.   But, notwithstand-
ing his love of academical retirement, he had now too
long enjoyed the pleasures and festivities of public
life, to return with a good will to academical poverty.

He had, however, better fortune than he expected,
and, if he lamented his condition like the historian,
better than he deserved.   He had, during his absence
in Germany, been appointed Latin secretary to King
Edward ; and by the interest of Gardiner, Bishop of
Winchester, he was instated in the same office under
Philip and Mary, with a salary of twenty pounds a
year.

Soon after his admission to his new employment, he
gave an extraordinary specimen of his abilities and diligence, by composing and transcribing with his usual
elegance, in three days, forty-seven letters to princes
and personages, of whom cardinals were the lowest.

How Ascham, who was known to be a Protestant,
could preserve the favor of Gardiner, and hold a place
of honor and profit in Queen Mary's court, it must be
very natural to inquire.   Cheke, as is well known, was
compelled to a recantation ; and why Ascham was
spared, cannot now be discovered.   Graunt, at the
time when the transactions of Queen Mary's reign
must have been well enough remembered, declares
that Ascham always made open profession of the re-
formed religion, and that Englesfield and others often

endeavored to incite Gardiner against him, but found their accusations rejected with contempt; yet he allows that suspicions, and charges of temporization and compliance, had somewhat sullied his reputation. The author of the Biographia Britannica conjectures that he owed his safety to his innocence and usefulness; that it would have been unpopular to attack a man so little liable to censure, and that the loss of his pen could not have been easily supplied. But the truth is, that morality was never suffered in the days of persecution to protect heresy; nor are we sure that Ascham was more clear from common failings than those who suffered more; and, whatever might be his abilities, they were not so necessary but Gardiner could have easily filled his place with another secretary. Nothing is more vain, than at a distant time to examine the motives of discrimination and partiality; for the inquirer, having considered interest and policy, is obliged at last to admit more frequent and more active motives of human conduct, caprice, accident, and private affections.

At that time, if some were punished, many were forborne; and of many, why should not Ascham happen to be one? He seems to have been calm and prudent, and content with that peace which he was suffered to enjoy, a mode of behavior that seldom fails to produce security. He had been abroad in the last years of King Edward, and had at least given no recent offence. He was certainly, according to his own opinion, not much in danger; for in the next year

he resigned his fellowship, which by Gardiner's favor
he had continued to hold, though not resident, and
married Margaret Howe, a young gentlewoman of a
good family.

He was distinguished in this reign by the notice of
Cardinal Pole, a man of great candor, learning, and
gentleness of manners, and particularly eminent for his
skill in Latin, who thought highly of Ascham's style ;
of which it is no inconsiderable proof, that when Pole
was desirous of communicating a speech made by himself as legate in parliament to the Pope, he employed
Ascham to translate it.

He is said to have been not only protected by the
officers of state, but favored and countenanced by
the queen herself, so that he had no reason of complaint in that reign of turbulence and persecution ;
nor was his fortune much mended, when, in 1558, his
pupil Elizabeth mounted the throne. He was continued in his former employment with the same stipend ;·
but though he was daily admitted to the presence of
the queen, assisted her private studies, and partook
of her diversions ; sometimes read to her in the learned
languages, and sometimes played with her at draughts
and chess, — he added nothing to his twenty pounds
a year but the prebend of Westwang, in the church of
York, which was given him the year following. His
fortune was therefore not proportionate to the rank
which his offices and reputation gave him, or to the
favor in which he seemed to stand with his mistress.
Of this parsimonious allotment, it is again a hopeless

search to inquire the reason. The queen was not naturally bountiful, and perhaps did not think it necessary to distinguish by any prodigality of kindness a man who had formerly deserted her, and whom she might still suspect of serving rather for interest than affection. Graunt exerts his rhetorical powers in praise of Ascham's disinterestedness and contempt of money, and declares, that, though he was often reproached by his friends with neglect of his own interest, he never would ask any thing, and inflexibly refused all presents which his office or imagined interest induced any to offer him. Cambden, however, imputes the narrowness of his condition to his love of dice and cock-fights; and Graunt, forgetting himself, allows that Ascham was sometimes thrown into agonies by disappointed expectations. It may be easily discovered from his "Scholemaster," that he felt his wants, though he might neglect to supply them; and we are left to suspect that he showed his contempt of money, only by losing at play. If this was his practice, we may excuse Elizabeth, who knew the domestic character of her servants, if she did not give much to him who was lavish of a little.

However he might fail in his economy, it were indecent to treat with wanton levity the memory of a man who shared his frailties with all, but whose learning or virtues few can attain, and by whose excellences many may be improved, while himself only suffered by his faults.

In the reign of Elizabeth, nothing remarkable is

known to have befallen him except that in 1563 he was invited by Sir Edward Sackville to write the "Scholemaster," a treatise on education, upon an occasion which he relates in the beginning of the book.

This work, though begun with alacrity, in hope of a considerable reward, was interrupted by the death of the patron, and afterwards sorrowfully and slowly finished in the gloom of disappointment, under the pressure of distress.   But of the author's disinclination or dejection, there can be found no tokens in the work, which is conceived with great vigor, and finished with great accuracy, and perhaps contains the best advice that was ever given for the study of languages.

This treatise he completed, but did not publish; for that poverty which in our days drives authors so hastily in such numbers to the press, in the time of Ascham, I believe, debarred them from it.   The printers gave little for a copy, and, if we may believe the tale of Raleigh's history, were not forward to print what was offered them for nothing.   Ascham's book, therefore, lay unseen in his study, and was at last dedicated to Lord Cecil by his widow.

Ascham never had a robust or vigorous body, and his excuse for so many hours of diversion was his inability to endure a long continuance of sedentary thought.   In the latter part of his life he found it necessary to forbear any intense application of the mind from dinner to bedtime, and rose to read and write early in the morning.   He was for some years hectically feverish, and, though he found some alleviation

of his distemper, never obtained a perfect recovery of
his health. The immediate cause of his last sickness
was too close application to the composition of a
poem, which he proposed to present to the queen on
the day of her accession. To finish this, he forbore
to sleep at his accustomed hours, till in December,
1568, he fell sick of a kind of lingering disease, which
Graunt has not named, nor accurately described. The
most afflictive symptom was want of sleep, which he
endeavored to obtain by the motion of a cradle.
Growing every day weaker, he found it vain to contend with his distemper, and prepared to die with the
resignation and piety of a true Christian. He was
attended on his death-bed by Gravet, vicar of St. Sep-
ulchre, and Dr. Nowel, the learned dean of St. Paul's,
who gave ample testimony to the decency and devotion of his concluding life. He frequently testified his
desire of that dissolution which he soon obtained.
His funeral sermon was preached by Dr. Nowel.

Roger Ascham died in the fifty-third year of his
age, at a time when, according to the general course of
life, much might yet have been expected from him, and
when he might have hoped for much from others : but
his abilities and his wants were at an end together ;
and who can determine whether he was cut off from
advantages, or rescued from calamities? He appears
to have been not much qualified for the improvement
of his fortune. His disposition was kind and social :
he delighted in the pleasures of conversation, and was
probably not much inclined to business. This may

be suspected from the paucity of his writings. He has left little behind him ; and of that little, nothing was published by himself but the " Toxophilus " and the account of Germany. " The Scholemaster " was printed by his widow ; and the epistles were collected by Graunt, who dedicated them to Queen Elizabeth, that he might have an opportunity of recommending his son, Giles Ascham, to her patronage. The dedication was not lost : the young man was made, by the queen's mandate, fellow of a college in Cambridge, where he obtained considerable reputation. What was the effect of his widow's dedication to Cecil is not known : it may be hoped that Ascham's works obtained for his family, after his decease, that support which he did not in his life very plenteously procure them.

Whether he was poor by his own fault, or the fault of others, cannot now be decided ; but it is certain that many have been rich with less merit. His philological learning would have gained him honor in any country ; and among us it may justly call for that reverence which all nations owe to those who first rouse them from ignorance, and kindle among them the light of literature. Of his manners nothing can be said but from his own testimony, and that of his contemporaries. Those who mention him allow him many virtues. His courtesy, benevolence, and liberality are celebrated ; and of his piety we have not only the testimony of his friends, but the evidence of his writings.

That his English works have been so long neglected,

is a proof of the uncertainty of literary fame. He was scarcely known as an author in his own language till Mr. Upton published his " Scholemaster " with learned notes. His other poems were read only by those few who delight in obsolete books ; but as they are now collected into one volume, with the addition of some letters never printed before, the public has an opportunity of recompensing the injury, and allotting Ascham the reputation due to his knowledge and his eloquence.

[Dr. Johnson also wrote a dedication for Bennet's edition. The chosen patron was a member of the noble family, whose " names are on the waters " of South Carolina. His hereditary title has been worthily borne in our own day by the seventh earl of Shaftesbury, who died in 1885. This short paper is worth copying, for that characteristic touch of Johnson's pen, — " formed Elizabeth to empire." — C.]

To the Right Hon. Anthony Ashley Cooper, Earl of Shaftesbury, Baron Ashley, Lord Lieutenant, and Custos Rutulorum of Dorsetshire, F. R. S.

My Lord, — Having endeavoured, by an elegant and useful edition, to recover the esteem of the public to an author undeservedly neglected, the only care which I now owe to his memory, is that of inscribing his works to a patron whose acknowledged eminence of character may awaken attention and attract regard.

I have not suffered the zeal of an editor so far to take possession of my mind, as that I should obtrude upon your lordship any productions unsuitable to the dignity of your rank or of your sentiments. Ascham was not only the chief ornament of a celebrated college, but visited foreign countries, frequented courts, and lived in familiarity with statesmen and princes; not only instructed scholars in literature, but formed Elizabeth to empire.

To propagate the works of such a writer will not be unworthy of your lordship's patriotism: for I know not what greater benefits you can confer on your country, than that of preserving worthy names from oblivion, by joining them with your own. I am, my lord, your lordship's most obliged, most obedient, and most humble servant,

JAMES BENNET.

CHAPTER II.

"The SCHOOLMASTER is a classical production in English, which may be placed by the side of its great Latin rivals, the Orator of Cicero and the Institutes of Quintilian." — I. D'ISRAELI.

"THE SCHOLEMASTER."

THIS is a book scarcely two-thirds as large as the volume which the reader now has in his hand. It is divided into two nearly equal parts. The first part is on "The bringing up of youth;" the second on "The ready way to the Latin tongue." The work is avowedly based upon a passage of Cicero (*De Oratore*, Book I. chap. xxxiv.), which has been thus translated : —

"But in my daily exercises, I used, when a youth, to adopt chiefly that method which I knew that Caius Carbo, my adversary, generally practised, which was, that having selected some nervous piece of poetry, or read over such a portion of a speech as I could retain in my memory, I used to declaim upon what I had been reading in other words, chosen with all the judgment that I possessed. . . . Afterwards I thought proper, and continued the practice at a rather more advanced age, to translate the orations of the best Greek orators; by fixing upon which, I gained this advantage, that while I rendered into Latin what I had read in Greek, I not only used the best words, and yet such as were of common occurrence, but also formed some words by imitation, which would be new to our countrymen, taking care, however, that they were unobjectionable."

We propose to give a few extracts from the work, rather to show the author's style than to furnish an abstract of his views on the best methods of teaching the languages. Those wishing to learn these, will, of course, refer to the book. A good edition, in the original spelling, without notes, is published as one of a series of " English Reprints " — price one shilling, Birmingham, England, 1870. An account of Ascham's method, compared with later theories and systems, can be found in " Essays on Educational Reformers," by Robert Herbert Quick, Cincinnati, 1879. Under some form or other, Ascham's suggestions are embodied in every successful attempt to teach a strange language, especially to adult pupils. It seems proper that Ascham should have a little space in the Chautauqua series, as several languages are successfully taught in the summer schools (Dr. Vincent's " Chautauqua Movement," p. 69).

Our extracts from " The Scholemaster " will be given in modern *spelling*, as more convenient to general readers. The " Preface to the Reader " gives at length the reasons that led the author to write his little book. Both for manner and matter, it seems worthy of being copied in full. The titlepage is given, as nearly as possible, in the original style and spelling.

An edition of " The Whole Works of Roger Ascham " was published in London, 1865, by Dr. Giles of Oxford.

THE

SCHOLEMASTER

Or plaine and perfite way of tea-
chyng children, to vnderſtand, write, and
ſpeake, in Latin tong, but ſpecially purpoſed
for the priuate brynging vp of youth in Ientle-
men and Noble mens houſes, and commodious
alſo for all ſuch, as haue forgot the Latin
tonge, and would, by themſelues, with-
out a Scholemaster, in ſhort tyme,
and with ſmall paines, recouer a
ſufficient habilite, to vnder-
stand, write, and
ſpeake Latin.

¶ By Roger Aſcham.

¶ *An.* 1 5 7 0.

AT LONDON.

Printed by Iohn Daye, dwelling
ouer Alderſgate.

¶ *Cum Gratia et Priuilegio Regiæ Maieſtatis,*
per Decennium.

"PREFACE TO THE READER.

"WHEN the great plague was at London, the year 1563, the Queen's Majesty, Queen Elizabeth, lay at her Castle of Windsor; where upon the tenth day of December, it fortuned, that in Sir William Cecil's chamber, her Highness's principal Secretary, there dined together these personages, M. Secretary himself, Sir William Peter, Sir J. Mason, D. Wotton, Sir Richard Sackville, Treasurer of the Exchequer, Sir Walter Mildmay, Chancellor of Exchequer, M. Haddon, Master of Requests, M. John Astely, Master of the Jewel House, M. Bernard Hampton, M. Nicasius, and I.

"Of which number, the most part were of her Majesty's most honorable Privy Council, and the rest serving her in very good place. I was glad then, and do rejoice yet to remember, that my chance was so happy to be there that day, in the company of so many wise and good men together, as hardly then could have been picked out again, out of all England besides.

"M. Secretary hath this accustomed manner; though his head be never so full of most weighty affairs of the realm, yet at dinner time he doth seem to lay them always aside; and findeth ever fit occasion to talk pleasantly of other matters, but most gladly of some matter of learning,

38

wherein he will courteously hear the mind of the meanest at his table.

" Not long after our sitting down, ' I have strange news brought me,' saith M. Secretary, ' this morning, that divers scholars of Eaton run away from the school for fear of a beating.' Whereupon M. Secretary took occasion to wish, that some more discretion were in many schoolmasters, in using correction, than commonly there is ; who many times punish rather the weakness of nature, than the fault of the scholar ; whereby many scholars, that might else prove well, be driven to hate learning before they know what learning meaneth ; and so are made willing to forsake their books, and be glad to be put to any other kind of living. M. Peter, as one somewhat severe of nature, said plainly, that the rod only was the sword, that must keep the school in obedience, and the scholar in good order. Mr. Wotton, a man mild of nature, with soft voice and few words, inclined to M. Secretary's judgment, and said, ' In mine opinion the schoolhouse should be indeed as it is called by name, the house of play and pleasure, and not of fear and bondage ; and as I do remember, so saith Socrates in one place of Plato. And therefore if a rod carry the fear of a sword, it is no marvel if those that be fearful of nature, choose rather to forsake the play, than to stand always within the fear of a sword in a fond [*foolish*] man's handling.'

" M. Mason, after his manner, was very merry with both parties, pleasantly playing both with the shrewd touches of many curst boys, and with the small discretion of many lewd schoolmasters.

" M. Haddon was fully of M. Peter's opinion, and said, that the best schoolmaster of our time was the greatest beater, and named the person. 'Though,' quoth I, 'it was his good fortune, to send from his school into the University one of the best scholars indeed of all our time, yet wise men do think, that that came to pass, rather by the great towardness of the scholar, than by the great beating of the master; and whether this be true or no, you yourself are best witness.' I said somewhat further in the matter, how, and why, young children were sooner allured by love than driven by beating, to attain good learning; wherein I was bolder to say my mind, because M. Secretary courteously provoked me thereunto; or else in such a company and surely in his presence, my wont is to be more willing to use mine ears, than to occupy my tongue.

"Sir Walter Mildmay, M. Astley, and the rest, said very little; only Sir Richard Sackville said nothing at all. After dinner I went up to read with the Queen's Majesty. We read then together in the Greek tongue, as I well remember, that noble oration of Demosthenes against Æschines, for his false dealing in his embassage to King Philip of Macadonie. Sir Richard Sackville came up soon after, and finding me in her Majesty's privy chamber, he took me by the hand, and carrying me to the window said: 'M. Ascham, I would not for a good deal of money have been this day absent from dinner; where, though I said nothing, yet I gave as good ear, and do consider as well the talk that passed, as any one did there. M. Secretary said very wisely, and most truly, that many young wits be driven to hate learning, before they know what learning is. I can be good witness to this myself; for a fond (*foolish*) schoolmaster, before I was fully fourteen years old, drave me so with fear of beating from all love of learning, that now, when I know what difference it is, to have learning, and to have little, or none at all, I feel it my greatest grief, and find it my greatest hurt that ever came to me, that it was my so ill chance, to light upon so lewd a schoolmaster. But feeling it is but in vain to lament things past, and also wisdom to look to things to come, surely, God willing, if God lend me life, I will make this my mishap some occasion of good hap to little Robert Sackville my son's son. For whose bringing up, I would gladly, if it so please you, use specially your good advice. I hear say you have a son much of his age; we will deal thus together: point you out a schoolmaster, who by your order shall teach my son and yours, and for all the rest, I will provide, yea though they three do cost me a couple of hundred pounds by year; and besides, you shall find me as fast a friend to you and yours, as perchance any you have.' Which promise the worthy gentleman surely kept with me until his dying day. We had then farther talk together of bringing-up of children, of the nature of quick and hard wits, of the right choice of a good wit, of fear, and love and teaching children. We passed from children and came to young men, namely gentlemen: we talked of their too much liberty to live as they lust; of their letting loose too soon to over much experience of ill, contrary to the good order of many good old Commonwealths of the Persians, and Greeks; of wit gathered, and good fortune gotten by some, only by experience without learning. And, lastly, he required of me very earnestly to show what I thought of the common going of English men into Italy.

" 'But,' saith he, 'because this place and this time will not suffer so long talk as these good matters require, therefore I pray you, at my request, and at your leisure, put in some order of writing the chief points of this our talk, concerning the right order of teaching, and honesty of living, for the good bringing-up of children and young men; and surely beside contenting me, you shall both please and profit very many others.' I made some excuse by lack of ability, and weakness of body. 'Well,' saith he, 'I am not now to learn what you can do; our dear friend, good M. Goodricke, whose judgment I could well believe, did once for all satisfy me fully therein. Again, I heard you say, not long ago, that you may thank Sir John Cheke for all the learning you have; and I know very well myself, that you did teach the Queen. And therefore, seeing God did bless you, to make you the scholar of the best master, and also the schoolmaster of the best scholar, that ever were in our time, surely, you should please God, benefit your country, and honest your own name, if you would take the pains to impart to others what you learned of such a master, and how you taught such a scholar. And in uttering the stuff ye received of the one, in declaring the order ye took with the other, ye shall never lack neither matter, nor manner, what to write nor how to write in this kind of argument.'

" I beginning some further excuse, suddenly was called to come to the Queen. The night following I slept little; my head was so full of this our former talk, and I so mindful somewhat to satisfy the honest request of so dear a friend. I thought to prepare some little treatise for a New Year's gift that Christmas; but, as it chanceth to busy builders, so, in building this my poor schoolhouse (the rather because the form of it is somewhat new, and differing from others), the work rose daily higher and wider than I thought it would at the beginning. And though it appear now, and be in very deed, but a small cottage, poor for the stuff, and rude for the workmanship; yet in going forward I found the site so good, as I was loath to give it over; but the making so costly, out-reaching my ability, as many times I wished that some one of those three, my dear friends, with full purses, Sir Tho. Smith, M. Haddon, or M. Watson had had the doing of it. Yet nevertheless, I myself spending gladly that little, that I gat at home by good Sir John Cheke, and that I borrowed abroad of my friend Sturmius, beside somewhat that was left me in reversion, by my old Mas-ters, Plato, Aristotle and Cicero, I have at last patched it up, as I could, and as you see. If the matter be mean, and meanly handled, I pray you bear both with me, and it; for never work went up in worse weather, with more lets and stops, than this poor schoolhouse of mine. Westminster-Hall can bear some witness, beside much weakness of body, but more trouble of mind, by some such sores, as grieved me to touch them myself; and therefore I purpose not to open them to others. And in the midst of outward injuries and inward cares, to increase them withal, good Sir Richard Sackville dieth, that worthy gentleman; 'That earnest favorer and furtherer of God's true Religion; that faithful servitor to his prince and country; a lover of learning, and all learned men; wise in all doings; courte-ous to all persons, showing spite to none, doing good to many; and as I well found, to me so fast a friend, as I never lost the like before.' When he was gone, my heart was dead; there was not one that wore a black gown for him, who carried a heavier heart for him than I; when he was gone, I cast this book away; I could not look upon it, but with weeping eyes, in remembering him, who was the only setter on, to do it; and would have been not only a glad commender of it, but also a sure and certain comfort to me and mine for it.

"Almost two years together, this book lay scattered and neglected, and had been quite given over of me, if the goodness of one had not given me some life and spirit again. God, the mover of goodness, prosper always him and his, as he hath many times comforted me and mine, and, I trust to God, shall comfort more and more. Of whom most justly I may say, and very oft, and always gladly I am wont to say, that sweet verse of Sophocles, spoken by Œdipus to worthy Theseus, 'For whatsoever I have, I have through thee, and through none other of living men.'

"This hope hath helped me to end this book; which if he allow, I shall think my labors well employed, and shall not much esteem the mislikings of any others. And I trust he shall think the better of it because he shall find the best part thereof to come out of his school whom he of all men loved and liked best. Yet some men, friendly enough of nature, but of small judgment in learning, do think I take too much pains, and spend too much time, in setting forth these children's affairs. But those good men were never brought up in Socrates' school, who saith plainly 'that no man goeth about a more godly purpose, than he that is mindful of the good bringing-up both of his own and other men's children.' Therefore I trust, good and wise men will think well of this my doing. And of others, that think otherwise, I will think myself, they are but men, to be pardoned for their folly, and pitied for their ignorance.

"In writing this book, I have had earnest respect to three special points, — truth of religion, honesty in living, right order in learning. In which three ways, I pray God, my poor children may diligently walk; for whose sake, as nature moved, and reason required, and necessity also somewhat compelled, I was the willinger to take these pains. For seeing at my death, I am not like to leave them any great store of living, therefore in my lifetime, I thought good to bequeath unto them, in this little book, as in my will and testament, the right way to good learning : which if they follow, with the fear of God, they shall very well come to sufficiency of living. I wish also, with all my heart, that young Mr. Robert Sackville may take that fruit of this labor, that his worthy grandfather purposed he should have done ; and if any other do take either profit or pleasure hereby, they have cause to thank Mr. Robert Sackville, for whom specially this my schoolmaster was provided. And one thing I would have the reader consider in reading this book, that because no schoolmaster hath charge of any child, before he enter into his school ; therefore I leaving all former care, of their good bringing up, to wise and good parents, as a matter not belonging to the schoolmaster, I do appoint this my schoolmaster then, and there to begin, where his office and charge beginneth. Which charge lasteth not long, but until the scholar be made able to go to the University, to proceed in logic, rhetoric, and other kinds of learning. Yet if my schoolmaster, for love he beareth to his scholar, shall teach him somewhat for his furtherance, and better judgment in learning, that may serve him seven years after in the University, he doth his scholar no more wrong, nor deserveth no worse name thereby, than he doth in London, who selling silk, or cloth, unto his friend, doth give him better measure than either his promise or bargain was.

" Farewell in Christ."

EXTRACTS FROM "THE SCHOLE-MASTER."

————

" WITH the common use of teaching and beating in common schools of England, I will not greatly contend; which if I did, it were but a small grammatical controversy, neither belonging to heresy nor treason, nor greatly touching God nor the Prince; although in very deed, in the end, the good or ill bringing up of children, doth as much serve to the good or ill service of God, our Prince, and our whole country, as any one thing doth beside.

" I do gladly agree with all good Schoolmasters in these points; to have children brought to good perfectness in learning; to all honesty in manners; to have all faults rightly amended; to have every vice severally corrected : but for the order and way that leadeth rightly to these points, we somewhat differ. For commonly, many schoolmasters, some, as I have seen, more, as I have heard tell, be of so crooked a nature, as, when they meet with a hard-witted scholar, they rather break him than bow him, rather mar him than mend him. For when the schoolmaster is angry with some other matter, then will he soonest fall to beat his scholar; and though he himself should be punished for his folly, yet must he beat some scholar for his pleasure, though there be no cause for him to do so, nor yet fault in the scholar to deserve so." . . .

"And one example, whether love or fear doth work more in a child for virtue and learning, I will gladly report, which may be heard with some pleasure, and followed with more profit. Before I went into *Germany*, I came to Brodegate in Leicestershire, to take my leave of that noble Lady *Jane Grey*, to whom I was exceeding much beholden. Her parents, the Duke and Duchess, with all the household, Gentlemen and Gentlewomen, were hunting in the Park. I found her in her chamber reading *Phædon Platonis* in Greek, and that with as much delight as some gentlemen would read a merry tale in *Bocacio*. After salutation, and duty done, with some other talk, I asked her why she would leave such pastime in the Park? Smiling, she answered me : ' I wist, all their sport in the Park is but a shadow to that pleasure that I find in *Plato*. Alas, good folk, they never felt what true pleasure meant.' 'And how came you, Madame,' quoth I, 'to this deep knowledge of pleasure, and what did chiefly allure you unto it; seeing, not many women, but very few men have attained thereunto?' 'I will tell you,' quoth she, 'and tell you a truth, which perchance ye will marvel at. One of the greatest benefits that ever God gave me, is that he sent me so sharp and severe Parents, and so gentle a schoolmaster. For when I am in presence of either father or mother, whether I speak, keep silence, sit, stand, or go, eat, drink, be merry, or sad, be sewing, playing, dancing, or doing any thing else, I must do it, as it were, in full weight, measure, and number, even so perfectly as God made the world, or else I am so sharply taunted, so cruelly threatened, yea, presently sometimes with pinches, nippes, and bobbes, and other ways, which I will not name, for the honor I bear them, so without measure, misordered that I think myself in hell, till time come that I must go to *M. Elmer*, who teacheth me so gently, so pleasantly, with such fair allurements to learning, that I think all the time nothing while I am with him. And when I am called from him, I fall on weeping, because whatsoever I do else but learning, is full of grief, trouble, fear, and wholly misliking unto me. And thus my book hath been so much my pleasure, and bringeth daily to me more pleasure and more, that in respect of it, all other pleasures, in very deed, be but trifles and troubles unto me.' I remember this talk gladly, both because it is so worthy of memory, and because also it was the last talk that ever I had, and the last time that ever I saw that noble and worthy lady."

"But I marvel the less, that these misorders be among some in the Court, for commonly in the country also everywhere, innocency is gone; Bashfulness is banished; much presumption in youth; small authority in age; Reverence is neglected; duties be confounded; and to be short, disobedience doth overflow the banks of good order, almost in every place, almost in every degree of man."

"This last summer, I was in a gentleman's house, where a young child, somewhat past four years old, could in no wise frame his tongue to say a little short grace: and yet he could roundly rap out so many ugly oaths, and those of the newest fashion, as some good man of fourscore years old hath never heard named before; and that which was most detestable of all, his father and mother would laugh at it. I much doubt what comfort,

another day, this child shall bring unto them. This Child
using much the company of serving men, and giving good
care to their talk, did easily learn which he shall hardly
forget all the days of his life hereafter: so likewise, in
the Court, if a young Gentleman will venture himself into
the company of Ruffians, it is over great a jeopardy, lest
their fashions, manners, thoughts, talk, and deeds will
very soon be ever like. The confounding of companies
breedeth confusion of good manners both in the Court
and everywhere else."

"These be the enchantments of *Circes*, brought out of
Italy, to mar men's manners in England; much, by example of ill life, but more by precepts of fond books, of
late translated out of *Italian* into English, sold in every
shop in London, commended by honest titles the sooner
to corrupt honest manners; dedicated over boldly to vir-
tuous and honorable personages, the more easily to beguile
simple and innocent wits. It is pity that those which
have authority and charge to allow and disallow books to
be printed, be no more circumspect herein than they are.
Ten Sermons at Paul's Cross do not so much good for
moving men to true doctrine, as one of those books do
harm, with enticing men to ill living. Yea I say farther,
those books tend not so much to corrupt honest living,
as they do to subvert true Religion."

"I had once a proof hereof, tried by good experience,
by a dear friend of mine, when I came first from Cambridge, to serve the Queen's Majesty, then Lady *Elizabeth*, lying at worthy Sir *Ant. Denys* in Cheston. *John
Whitney*, a young gentleman, was my bed-fellow, who
willing by good nature and provoked by mine advice,

began to learn the Latin tongue, after the order declared in this book. We began after Christmas : I read unto him *Tullie de Amicitia*, which he did every day twice translate, out of Latin into English, and out of English into Latin again. About St. Lawrence-tide [1] after, to prove how he profited, I did choose out *Torquatus'* talk *de Amicitia* in the latter end of the first book *de finib.*, because that place was the same in matter, like in words and phrases, nigh to the form and fashion of sentences, as he had learned before in *de Amicitia*. I did translate it myself into plain English, and gave it him to turn into Latin : which he did, so choicely, so orderly, so without any great miss in the hardest points of Grammar, that some, in seven years in Grammar Schools, yea, and some in the Universities too, cannot do half so well. This worthy young Gentleman, to my greatest grief, to the great lamentation of that whole house, and specially to that most noble Lady, now Queen *Elizabeth* herself, departed within few days, out of this world.

"And if in any cause a man may without offence of God speak somewhat ungodly, surely, it was some grief unto me, to see him hie so hastily to God, as he did. A Court full of such young Gentlemen, were rather a Paradise than a Court upon earth. And though I had never Poetical head, to make any verse, in any tongue, yet either love, or sorrow, or both, did wring out of me then, certain careful thoughts of my good will towards him, which in my mourning for him, fell forth, more by chance, than either by skill or use, into this kind of misorderly metre : —

"My own John Whitney, now farewell, now death doth part us twain.
No death, but parting for a while, whom life shall join again.
Therefore my heart, cease sighs and sobs, cease sorrow's seed to sow,
Whereof no gain, but greater grief, and hurtful care may grow.

[1] [August 10.]

Yet, when I think upon such gifts of grace as God him lent,
My loss, his gain, I must awhile, with joyful tears lament.
Young years to yield such fruit in Court, where seed of vice is sown,
Is sometimes read, in some place seen, amongst us seldom known.
His life he led, Christ's lore to learn, with will to work the same:
He read to know, and knew to live, and lived to praise his name.
So fast to friend, so foe to few, so good to every wight,
I may well wish, but scarcely hope, again to have in sight.
The greater joy his life to me, his death the greater pain:
His life in Christ so surely set, doth glad my heart again:
His life so good, his death better, do mingle mirth with care,
My spirit with joy, my flesh with grief, so dear a friend to spare.
Thus God the good, while they be good, doth take and leaves us ill,
That we should mend our sinful life, in life to tarry still.
Thus, we well left, be better reft, in heaven to take his place,
That by like life, and death, at last, we may obtain like grace.
My own John Whitney, again farewell, awhile thus part in twain,
Whom pain doth part in earth, in heaven, great joy shall join again."

"And here, for my pleasure I purpose a little, by the way, to play and sport with my master *Tully*, from whom commonly I am never wont to dissent. He himself, for this point of learning, in his verses doth halt a little by his leave. He could not deny it, if he were alive, nor those defend him now that love him best. This fault I lay to his charge; because once it pleased him, though somewhat merrily, yet over uncourteously, to rail upon poor England, objecting both extreme beggary and mere barbarousness unto it, writing thus unto his friend *Atticus:* 'There is not one scruple of silver in that whole Isle, or any one that knoweth either learning or letter.'

"But now, master *Cicero*, blessed be God and His son, Jesus Christ, whom you never knew, except it were as it pleased him to lighten you by some shadow, as covertly in one place ye confess saying, '*Veritatis tantum um-*

bram confectamur,' as your master, *Plato*, did before
you : blessed be God, I say, that sixteen hundred year
after you were dead and gone, it may truly be said, that
for silver there is more comely plate in one city of England than is in four of the proudest Cities in all *Italy*, and
take *Rome* for one of them. And for learning, beside the
knowledge of all learned tongues and liberal sciences,
even your own books, *Cicero*, be as well read, and your
excellent eloquence is as well liked and loved, and as
truly followed in England at this day as it is now, or ever
was, since your own time, in any place of *Italie*, either at
Arpinum, where you were born, or else at *Rome*, where
ye were brought up. And a little to brag with you, *Cicero*,
where you yourself, by your leave, halted in some point
of learning in your own tongue ; many in England at this
'day go straight up, both in true skill and right doing
therein."

"SALLUST.

"*Sallust* is a wise and worthy writer, but he requireth
a learned Reader, and a right considerer of him. My dearest friend, and best master that ever I had or heard in
learning, Sir *J. Cheke*, such a man, as if I should live to
see England breed the like again, I fear I should live
over long, did once give me a lesson for Sallust, which I
shall never forget myself, so it is worthy to be remembered of all those that would come to perfect judgment
of the Latin tongue. He said that *Sallust* was not very
fit for young men to learn out of him the purity of the
Latin tongue, because he was not the purest in propriety
of words, nor choicest in aptness of phrases, nor the best
in framing of sentences ; and therefore is his writing, said
he, neither plain for the matter, nor sensible for men's

understanding. 'And what is the cause thereof, sir?'
Quoth I. 'Verily,' said he, 'because in *Sallust's* writing
is more Art than nature, and more labor than art; and in
his labor also, too much toil, as it were, with an uncon-
tented care to write better than he could, a fault common
to very many men. And, therefore, he doth not express
the matter lively and naturally with common speech as ye
see *Zenophon* doth in Greek, but it is carried and driven
forth artificially, after so learned a sort, as *Thucydides*
doth in his orations.' 'And how cometh it to pass,' said
I, 'that *Cæsar's* and *Cicero's* talk is so natural and plain,
and Sallust's writing so artificial and dark, when all they
three lived in one time?' 'I will freely tell you my fancy
herein,' said he: 'surely *Cæsar* and *Cicero*, beside a singular prerogative of natural eloquence given unto them
by God, both two, by use of life, were daily orators
among the common people, and greatest counsellors in
the Senate house; and therefore gave themselves to use
such speech as the meanest should well understand, and
the wisest best allow, following carefully that good counsel
of *Aristotle*, "*loquendum ut multi, sapiendum ut pauci.*"
Sallust was no such man, neither for will to goodness, nor
skill by learning; but ill given by nature, and made worse
by bringing up, spent the most part of his youth very
misorderly in riot and revelling. In the company of such,
who, never giving their mind to honest doing, could never
inure their tongue to wise speaking. But at the last coming to better years, and buying wit at the dearest hand,
that is, by long experience of the hurt and shame that
cometh of mischief, moved by the counsel of them that
were wise, and carried by the example of such as were
good, first fell to honesty of life, and after to the love to
study and learning; and so became so new a man, that

Cæsar being dictator, made him prætor in *Numidia*, where he, absent from his country, and not inured with the common talk of Rome, but shut up in his study, and bent wholly to reading, did write the story of the Romans.'"

MEMOIR

OF

THOMAS ARNOLD

OF RUGBY, ENGLAND,

WITH SPECIAL REFERENCE TO HIS LIFE AND WORK AS A TEACHER.

SELECTED FROM

LIFE AND CORRESPONDENCE,

BY

ARTHUR PENRHYN STANLEY.

(ORIGINALLY PUBLISHED IN LONDON IN 1845.)

WITH AN INTRODUCTION

BY

JAMES H. CARLISLE,

PRESIDENT OF WOFFORD COLLEGE, SPARTANBURG, S.C.

BOSTON:
CHAUTAUQUA PRESS,
117 FRANKLIN STREET.
1886.

THOMAS ARNOLD.

. . . "One of the noblest minds and highest characters of these days — prematurely taken from us, in the middle of a career of usefulness which we believe we are guilty of no extravagance in terming unparalleled in the line of life which Dr. Arnold adopted." — GLADSTONE, *January, 1843.*

"We never recollect a religious life which so much affected us; which, while reading, we wished so much to make our own; revolving which, we can so little justify ourselves that it shall not be so." — EDINBURGH REVIEWER, *January, 1845.*

INTRODUCTION.

ASCHAM, in a letter dated in 1550, laments the ruin of grammar schools in England, and predicts, "from their decline, the speedy extinction of the universities." This sentence may give us a slight connection between the names of Ascham and Arnold. In 1567, the year before Ascham's death, Laurence Sheriff, a London grocer, dying, left a small amount of property to found a grammar school in Rugby, his native town, about eighty miles north-west of London. This was a small place (now containing eight thousand inhabitants) in Warwickshire, an agricultural county. The property was chiefly in real estate in London, yielding at first only the value of a few hundred dollars yearly. With the growth of the city the property improved, until, in the first part of this century, it annually yielded more than twenty thousand dollars. The school, of course, also improved in some respects; but it did not rank with the leading high schools, as Eton and Westminster. A writer in "The Edinburgh Review" (January, 1845) says that twenty years before that date Rugby "was the lowest and most Bœotian of the

English schools." To-day its name is a household word all over the English world. In East Tennessee we have an English town bearing the familiar name. All this sudden importance is due to the life, labors, and biography of the man who was the head master there from 1828 to 1842. He followed Dr. Wool ; and he was followed by Dr. A. C. Tait, who rose to be archbishop of Canterbury. But the name of Thomas Arnold is better known to general readers than that of either of these distinguished men. The present head master is Dr. T. W. Jex-Blake, who has twenty-one assistants.

He is a bold man who will undertake to improve Stanley's " Life of Arnold," or even to condense it in just proportion. Neither of these tasks is attempted here. Such portions of the work have been taken as serve to show Arnold's work and life as a teacher. This could be done only by leaving out much valuable matter. The first chapter, giving his life up to the close of his university course, is given entire. From the second chapter, containing his life as a private tutor preparing pupils for the university, a page or two of Stanley's text and some of Arnold's letters have been omitted. The famous third chapter, with its full record of his Rugby life, is given at length, the foot-notes only being omitted. This chapter is long, and out of proportion to the size of the memoir ; but no careful reader will wish that a page had been left out. Of the fourth chapter, that portion which describes Arnold's domestic life is retained, with specimens of his letters. The five following chapters, with letters appended to each, are omitted entirely. Our fifth chapter gives a portion of the last (tenth) chapter in the original work. It contains a short reference to the historical lectures at Oxford, while the touching account of Arnold's death is given at length. This should never be mutilated or abridged. The late Francis Lieber, speaking to a pupil about that portion of the biography, said, literally with tears in his eyes, " His death was beautiful." Nothing has been added to the work as Stanley wrote it ; and (except in a single instance, where it seemed necessary to keep the connection by joining two sentences, omitting a few words in one) not a sentence or a word has been changed. Throughout this memoir, the reader may know that he has the literal words of the original work, of which scarcely one-fourth is here given.

Arnold died in 1842 ; and his biography first appeared in 1845, when the first edition was published in London. Happy alike in its subject and in its author, the work at once attracted attention in the reading-world. It was translated into several foreign languages. Perhaps it may be said to mark an era in the art of writing biographies. In America, several editions appeared in Boston and New York. It was noticed in the leading reviews of that day. The different religious magazines all agreed in praising the skill of the biographer, while each found something to approve and admire in Arnold's character and life. From the nature of the case, many of the readers of

the book had never heard of Thomas Arnold until
after he was dead.   It is not strange that many of his
countrymen did not fully appreciate him while he was
with them.   "Chambers's Encyclopædia of English
Literature" was published after Arnold's death, but its
earlier editions do not contain his name.   It is true,
the genius of Stanley made his teacher more widely
known than he had been during his life.   But the
enthusiastic and discriminating biographer was un-
usually fortunate in his subject.   The interest created
by the work in our country was not transient.   From
year to year, it was noticed in the different literary and
religious periodicals.   In 1856 a very appreciative
review appeared in Barnard's "American Journal of
Education" by Professor Eliot of Trinity College,
Connecticut.   This was accompanied by a likeness,
which gave American readers their first view of
Arnold's fine English face.

There arose, of necessity, a demand for some of the
writings of the great Rugby teacher.   His inaugural
lectures at Oxford appeared in New York, with notes
by Professor Reed, in 1845.   A volume of miscella-
nies and three volumes of sermons were also republished.   In 1856 another of Arnold's pupils showed
to the world a lifelike view of their beloved friend
and teacher.   Thomas Hughes gave to all English-
reading boys a lasting treasure in "Tom Brown at
Rugby."   This little book seems likely to go down to
the next generation, stirring the hearts of the school-
boys everywhere, and helping them to lead pure and

manly lives. A few months ago the " St. Nicholas "
magazine had two illustrated articles on Rugby School,
which were, no doubt, welcome to thousands who wish
to see the places and the games associated in their
pleasant memories of "Tom and Arthur."

More than forty years have passed since Stanley's
work first appeared. Every generation has its own
heroes, and its own biographies, bearing the " form
and pressure of the times." Not many biographies go
down to a second or third generation of readers. A
magazine of February, 1886, has a list of special works
of the kind, recommended to young ministers by Dr.
Lyman Abbot. Among them are, Boswell's " Life of
Johnson," and Stanley's " Life of Arnold." There
seems to be a place still in our current literature for
this standard work. Several circumstances may com-
bine to give it room among books that are now read.
The visits of Dean Stanley, Matthew Arnold, and
Thomas Hughes to our country, and the Rugby colony
of Englishmen, may have this effect in some degree.
The popularity of "Tom Brown" will certainly prepare the way. Many boys who have cried with "Tom "
because his fishing-frolic on that summer day in 1842
was so sadly brought to an end, will wish to learn
something more about the man over whose grave their
young hero stood and wept. This little memoir will
do its desired work in the case of every reader who
lays it down, wishing to read the large biography. It
is an era in the history of any young teacher when he
becomes familiar with the " Life of Thomas Arnold."

This will suggest a special reason why such a volume may appropriately find its place in our educational literature. Many young teachers are eagerly searching for books to help them in their daily work. Teachers' institutes are common. Teachers' reading-circles are formed in many communities. These are all encouraging signs. They make it the more important, that our teachers shall be guarded against some common mistakes. There are so many helps just now for them, they may be led to think that good teaching, in the widest sense, is an art that can be readily taught by an expert. They must be reminded that there is no short or royal road to good teaching, other than the king's highway of good living. He who wishes to teach well, must, first of all, try to live well. He who wishes to do something in his chosen life-work, must aim to be something. He who wishes to *have* a good influence, must first *be* a good influence. To teach a child to read, to write, to cipher, is something. It may be a great deal. But to teach him to live is far more. To think, to reason, to love truth, and to search for truth; to love the right, and pursue it, alone if need be; to love all that is lovely, and to hate only that which is hateful, — this is not so easy as to turn Latin into English, or to do problems in algebra. All this the teacher of to-day may forget in his search after technical skill in handling the machinery of the school-room, or in his haste to prepare the boy for a close competitive examination. He may be satisfied if he gives the boy some outside finish, as the barber is satisfied if, cutting the boy's hair, he "turns out a nice job." No fresh work in pedagogics can render the record of a life like Arnold's useless. Here is an object-lesson, which the teachers of this generation and the next may study with growing interest. Let all labor-saving and labor-utilizing expedients be multiplied in the schoolroom. Make your educational machinery as ingenious and as effective as possible. But the vital question still recurs, "What force is to move all this?" The teacher is greater than all machinery, and the man is greater than the teacher. The teacher is only one side of the man. Without regard to the routine or usages of Rugby School, the life of the Rugby teacher will quicken and help every other teacher. Let us take a few extracts from letters not published in this memoir : —

"The school will become more and more engrossing; and so it ought to be, for it is impossible ever to do enough in it. Yet I think it essential that I should not give up my own reading, as I always find any addition of knowledge always to turn to account for the school in some way or other."

"Meantime, I write nothing, and read barely enough to keep my mind in the state of a running stream, which I think it ought to be, if it would form and feed other minds; for it is ill drinking out of a pond whose stock of water is merely the remains of the long-past rains of the winter and spring, evaporating and diminishing with every successive day of drought."

"A schoolmaster's intercourse is with the young, the strong, and the happy; and he cannot get on with them, unless in animal spirits he can sympathize with them, and show them that his thoughtfulness is not connected with selfishness and weakness."

As this short memoir is taken up wholly with Arnold as a teacher, it may be well to refer here briefly to other sides of his strong character, which are fully brought out in the biography. He was a preacher, and the author of several volumes of published sermons. He lived at a time when the religious mind of the Established Church and of other circles was deeply stirred. Arnold could not be either a neutral or a partisan on any important question. He could doubt, or suspend his opinion, but he could not be indifferent. We have nothing to do now with his peculiar views as a theologian. Our only purpose is to call attention to the style and general spirit of his sermons. His first volume was published in 1828, soon after reaching Rugby. In the preface he says, —

"My object has been, to bring the great principles of the gospel home to the hearts and practices of my own countrymen, in my own time, and particularly to those of my own station in society, with whose sentiments and language I am naturally most familiar. And for this purpose, I have tried to write in such a style as might be used in real life, in serious conversation with our friends, or with those who asked our advice; in the language, in short, of common life, and applied to the cases of common life, but ennobled and strengthened by those principles and feelings which are to be found only in the gospel."

Might not these words stand as an exact description of the style of some great evangelists who just now are drawing the multitudes after them?

Julius Hare says of Arnold, as a preacher, "I do

not mean to profess an entire agreement with all his opinions : on many points we differed more or less ; but whether differing or agreeing, when I turn from the ordinary theological or religious writers of the day, to one of his volumes, there is a feeling, as it were, of breathing the fresh mountain air after having been shut up in the morbid atmosphere of a sick-room, or in the fumigated vapors of an Italian church."

Arnold was an intelligent Englishman, a devoted lover of his country and its free institutions. He finished his university course in the memorable year in which the battle of Waterloo was fought. His whole life was covered by a season of excitement and commotion in English history. Two years before his death, he wrote to a friend, " The state of the times is so grievous, that it really pierces through all private happiness, and haunts me daily like a personal calamity." He felt much, thought much, and wrote much on public questions. He paid the usual, perhaps the inevitable, penalty of having strong personal convictions. He was not spared that discipline which puts the finest finish to heart and character. He was misunderstood and reviled. When assailed, he could not utter the party pass-word which brings eager clansmen to the relief. He spoke on the subject of parties, with an earnestness not easily understood by many then or now. For example : Writing to a friend in 1833, he says, " May God grant to my sons, if they live to manhood, an unshaken love of truth, and a firm resolution to follow it for themselves, with an intense abhorrence of all party ties, save that one tie which binds them to the party of Christ against wickedness ! ' Again, in one of his sermons, —

" Be of one party to the death, and that is Christ's; but abhor every other. Abhor it; that is, as a thing to which to join yourselves : for every party is mixed up of good and evil, of truth and falsehood; and in joining it, therefore, you join with the one as well as the other. If circumstances should occur which oblige you practically to act with any one party, as the least of two evils, then watch yourselves the more lest the least of two evils should, by any means, commend itself at last to your mind as a positive good. Join it with a sad and reluctant heart, protesting against its evil, dreading its victory, far more pleased to serve it by suffering than by acting; for it is in Christ's cause only that we can act with heart and soul, as well as patiently and triumphantly suffer. Do this amidst reproach and suspicion and cold friendship and zealous enmity; for this is the portion of those who seek to follow their Master, and him only. Do it, although your foes be they of your own household, those whom nature or habit or choice had once bound to you most closely. And then you will understand how, even now, there is a daily cross to be taken up by those who seek not to please men, but God; yet you will learn no less how that cross, meekly and firmly borne, whether it be the cross of men's ill opinion from without, or of our own evil nature struggled against within, is now, as ever, peace and wisdom and sanctification and redemption through him who first bore it."

Arnold published a critical edition of Thucydides, and was writing a history of Rome. He was planning, for many years, a work on " Church and State," or " Christian Politics," which is touchingly alluded to in the last lines traced by his pen, a few hours before his death. While in the "full activity of zeal and power," he fell in his prime. Two years before his death, a friend called his attention to the fact that a number of prominent men had died at the age of forty-seven (Philip of Macedon, Addison, William Jones, Nelson, Pitt), and said to him, "Beware of your forty-seventh year." He died at that age. When Stephen Olin learned from an item in a newspaper of Arnold's death, he said, with emotion, "I am just at the age at which he died." When he read Stanley's "Life," a year or two later, he was moved to tears. These two great men lived in different continents, moved in different religious circles, and never met. They had much in common, added to their kindred pursuits as devoted teachers. They were alike in the plain simplicity and great purity of life and character, and in their deep love and loyalty to Him whose name was so often on their lips in prayer and praise.

Such are a few points in the history of the man whose life is so lovingly and so truthfully portrayed by the hand of his pupil. It seems appropriate every way that the increasing Chautauquan brotherhood should be invited to study the life of one who took an abiding interest in the welfare of all classes, and in all kindly intercourse between the rich and poor. If alive to-day in our midst, we may well believe that Arnold would give his aid to an enterprise which aims to further these great ends. Cheap, safe reading for the masses was a great desire with him. He once wrote to a friend, "I never wanted articles on religious subjects half so much as articles on common subjects, written with a decidedly Christian tone."

Stanley's life was greatly influenced by Arnold; and nobly has he, at least, recognized a debt which never can be fully repaid. It is touching now to read the letters of his anxious mother, when seeking a good school for her timid, bright little Arthur. She was advised to write to the new head master at Rugby. She did so, and the answer satisfied her: she had met "the teacher who would take kindly to Arthur, and to whom Arthur would take kindly." Arthur was sent away to school; and in a few months, of course, the *child-sick* mother must visit the *home-sick* boy. Here is a passage worth quoting from her pen: —

"March, 1829. — We went to dine with Dr. and Mrs. Arnold; and they are of the same opinion, that Arthur was as well off and as happy as he could be at a public school: and, on the whole, I am satisfied, — quite satisfied, considering all things, — for Dr. and Mrs. Arnold are indeed delightful. She was ill, but still animated and lively. He has a very remarkable countenance, something in forehead, and again in manner, which puts me in mind of Reginald Heber; and there is a mixture of zeal, energy, and determination, tempered with wisdom, candor, and benevolence, both in manner and in every thing he says. He had examined Arthur's class, and said Arthur had done very well, and the class generally. He said he was gradually reforming, but that it was like pasting down a piece of paper, — as fast as one corner was put down, another started up. 'Yes,' said Mrs. A., 'but Dr. Arnold always thinks the corner will not start *again.*' And it is that happy, sanguine temperament which is so particularly calculated to do well in this, or indeed any, situation." — Augustus J. C. Hare.

Arthur must have done very well on more than one occasion. He took five medals, all that were open to him in his Rugby course. When delivering the last, the teacher quietly handed it to him, saying, "Thank you, Stanley: we have nothing more to give you." Stanley carried away from Rugby that which is better than all medals, or even than all scholarship. He had, for life, an intense admiration for goodness and truth, as he had seen them embodied. At thirty years of age he wrote the great biography, which, if he had written nothing else, would give him a high place in English literature. More than thirty other publications of all sizes show his industry and zeal. His theological views are not now before us, for passing words of either praise or blame. His name will be long associated with that of his great teacher. When in Baltimore, in 1878, Dean Stanley said, in a public address, "The lapse of years has only served to deepen in me the conviction that no gift can be more valuable than the recollection and inspiration of a great character working on our own. I hope you may all experience this at some time in your life, as I have done." On his death-bed, three years later, he said of Westminster Abbey, "I have labored amidst many frailties, and with much weakness, to make this institution more and more the great centre of religious and national life in a truly liberal spirit." That rich fruit was from seed planted at Rugby.

An admirable little volume of Stanley's quotable passages has been recently published by Lothrop &

Co., Boston. In it, a specimen of Stanley's handwriting is given in *facsimile*, very unlike the hand which Roger Ascham would have taught him. The sentence is this : —

" It will be a great pleasure to me if any words of mine can assist the rising generation of the United States to fulfil the duties, and solve the problems, of the age in which we live."

Let many young teachers in this generation come within the spell of Stanley's admiration for Arnold. Let our colleges and schools be filled with men, who, in their sphere, will try to catch the spirit of Arnold's life. Pupils taught by such men will scarcely fail to seek for the blessing of God upon themselves and their generation. With that blessing, we may hope they will be ready in some good degree to solve the problems, and to meet the unanswered questions, which the twentieth century will very soon lay before them.

JAS. H. CARLISLE.

Spartanburg, S.C., April 20, 1886.

LIFE OF THOMAS ARNOLD, D.D.

CHAPTER I.

EARLY LIFE AND EDUCATION.

THOMAS ARNOLD, seventh child and youngest son of William and Martha Arnold, was born on June 13, 1795, at West Cowes, in the Isle of Wight, where his family had been settled for two generations, their original residence having been at Lowestoff, in Suffolk.

His father, who was collector of the customs at Cowes, died suddenly of spasm in the heart, on March 3, 1801. His two elder brothers, William and Matthew, died, the first in 1806, the second in 1820. His sisters all survived him, with the exception of the third, Susannah, who, after a lingering complaint in the spine, died at Laleham, in 1832.

His early education was confided by his mother to her sister, Miss Delafield, who took an affectionate pride in her charge, and directed all his studies as a child. In 1803 he was sent to Warminster School, in Wiltshire, under Dr. Griffiths, with whose assistant master, Mr. Lawes, he kept up his intercourse long after they had parted. In 1807 he was removed to Winchester, where, having entered as a commoner, and afterwards become a scholar of the college, he remained till 1811. In after-life he always cherished a strong Wykehamist feeling, and, during his head-mastership at Rugby, often recurred to his knowledge, there first acquired, of the peculiar constitution of a public school, and to his recollection of the tact in managing boys shown by Dr. Goddard, and the skill in imparting scholarship which distinguished Dr. Gabell, who, during his stay there, were successively head masters of Winchester.

He was then, as always, of a shy and retiring disposition ; but his manner as a child, and till his entrance at Oxford, was marked by a stiffness and formality the very reverse of the joyousness and simplicity of his later years : his family and schoolfellows both remember him as unlike those of his own age, and with peculiar pursuits of his own ; and the tone and style of his early letters, which have been for the most part preserved, are such as might naturally have been produced by living chiefly in the company of his elders, and reading, or hearing read to him before he could read himself, books suited to a more advanced age. His boyish friendships were strong and numerous. It is needless here to enumerate the names of those Winchester schoolfellows of whose after-years it was the pride and delight to watch the course of their companion through life ; but the fond recollections, which were long cherished on both sides, of his intercourse with his earliest friend at Warminster, of whom he saw and heard nothing from that time till he was called upon in 1829 to write his epitaph, is worth recording, as a remarkable instance of strong impressions of nobleness of character, early conceived and long retained.

Both as a boy and a young man he was remarkable for a difficulty in early rising, amounting almost to a constitutional infirmity ; and though his after-life will show how completely this was overcome by habit, yet he often said that early rising was a daily effort to him, and that in this instance he never found the truth of the usual rule, that all things are made easy by custom. With this, however, was always united great occasional energy ; and one of his schoolfellows gives it as his impression of him, that "he was stiff in his opinions, and utterly immovable by force or fraud, when he made up his mind, whether right or wrong."

It is curious to trace the beginnings of some of his later interests in his earliest amusements and occupations. He never lost the recollection of the impression produced upon him by the excitement of naval and military affairs, of which he naturally saw and heard much by living at the Isle of Wight in the time of the war ; and the sports in which he took most pleasure, with the few playmates of his childhood, were in sailing rival fleets in his father's garden, or acting the battles of the Homeric heroes, with whatever imple-

ments he could use as spear and shield, and reciting
their several speeches from Pope's translation of the
Iliad. He was from his earliest years exceedingly
fond of ballad poetry, which his Winchester schoolfellows used to learn from his repetition before they
had seen it in print; and his own compositions as a
boy all ran in the same direction. A play of this kind,
in which his schoolfellows were introduced as the
dramatis personæ, and a long poem of "Simon de
Montfort," in imitation of Scott's Marmion, procured
for him at school, by way of distinction from another
boy of the same name, the appellation of Poet Arnold.
And the earliest specimen of his composition which
has been preserved is a little tragedy, written before
he was seven years old, on "Piercy, Earl of Northum-
berland," suggested apparently by Home's play of
"Douglas;" which, however, contains nothing worthy
of notice, except, perhaps, the accuracy of orthography,
language, and blank-verse metre, in which it is written,
and the precise arrangement of the different acts and
scenes.

But he was most remarked for his forwardness in
history and geography. His strong power of memory
(which, however, in later years depended mainly on
association), extending to the exact state of the weather
on particular days, or the exact words and position of
passages which he had not seen for twenty years,
showed itself very early, and chiefly on these subjects.
One of the few recollections which he retained of his
father was, that he received from him, at three years

old, a present of Smollett's "History of England," as a reward for the accuracy with which he had gone through the stories connected with the portraits and pictures of the successive reigns ; and, at the same age, he used to sit at his aunt's table, arranging his geographical cards, and recognizing by their shape, at a glance, the different counties of the dissected map of England.

He long retained a grateful remembrance of the miscellaneous books to which he had access in the school library at Warminster ; and when, in his professorial chair at Oxford, he quoted Dr. Priestley's "Lectures on History," it was from his recollection of what he had there read when he was eight years old. At Winchester he was a diligent student of Russell's "Modern Europe ;" Gibbon and Mitford he had read twice over before he left school ; and amongst the comments on his reading, and the bursts of political enthusiasm on the events of the day in which he indulged in his Winchester letters, it is curious, as connected with his later labors, to read his indignation when fourteen years old, "at the numerous boasts which are everywhere to be met with in the Latin writers." "I verily believe," he adds, "that half at least of the Roman history is, if not totally false, at least scandalously exaggerated : how far different are the modest, unaffected, and impartial narrations of Herodotus, Thucydides, and Xenophon."

The period, both of his home and school education, was too short to exercise much influence upon his after-life. But he always looked back upon it with a marked tenderness. The keen sense which he entertained of the bond of relationship and of early association — not the less from the blank in his own domestic recollections occasioned by his father's death, and his own subsequent removal from the Isle of Wight —invested with a peculiar interest the scenes and companions of his childhood. His strong domestic affections had acted as an important safeguard to him, when he was thrown at so early an age into the new sphere of an Oxford life; and when, in later years, he was left the head of the family, he delighted in gathering round him the remains of his father's household, and in treasuring up every particular relating to his birthplace and parentage, even to the graves of the older generations of the family in the parish church at Lowestoff, and the great willow-tree in his father's grounds at Slattwoods, from which he transplanted shoots successively to Laleham, to Rugby, and to Fox How. Every date in the family history, with the alteration of hereditary names, and the changes of their residence, was carefully preserved for his children in his own handwriting; and when in after-years he fixed on the abode of his old age in Westmoreland, it was his great delight to regard it as a continuation of his own early home in the Isle of Wight. And when, as was his wont, he used to look back from time to time over the whole of this period, it was with the solemn feeling which is expressed in one of his later journals, written on a visit to the place of his earliest school-

education, in the interval between the close of his
life at Laleham and the beginning of his work at
Rugby. " Warminster, January 5th [1828]. I have not
written this date for more than twenty years; and how
little could I foresee when I wrote it last, what would
happen to me in the interval. And now to look forward twenty years — how little can I guess of that
also. Only may He in whose hands are time and eternity, keep me evermore His own ; that whether I live,
I may live unto Him ; or whether I die, I may die
unto Him ; may He guide me with His counsel, and
after that receive me to glory, through Jesus Christ
our Saviour."

In 1811, in his sixteenth year, he was elected as a
scholár at Corpus Christi College, Oxford ; in 1814
his name was placed in the first class in Litteræ Hu-
maniores ; in the next year he was elected Fellow of
Oriel College ; and he gained the Chancellor's prize
for the two University essays, Latin and English, for
the years 1815 and 1817. Those who know the influence which his college friendships exercised over his
after-life, and the deep affection which he always bore
to Oxford, as the scene of the happiest recollections
of his youth, and the sphere which he hoped to occupy
with the employments of his old age, will rejoice in the
possession of the following record of his undergraduate
life by that true and early friend, to whose timely advice, protection, and example, at the critical period

when he was thrown with all the spirits and the inexperience of boyhood on the temptations of the university, he always said and felt, that he had owed more than to any other man in the world.

LETTER FROM MR. JUSTICE COLERIDGE.

HEATH'S COURT, September, 1843.

MY DEAR STANLEY, — When you informed me of Mrs. Arnold's wish that I would contribute to your memoir of our dear friend, Dr. Arnold, such recollections as I had of his career as an undergraduate at Oxford, with the intimation that they were intended to fill up that chapter in his life, my only hesitation in complying with her wish arose from my doubts whether my impressions were so fresh and true, or my powers of expression such, as to enable me to do justice to the subject. A true and lively picture of him at that time would be, I am sure, interesting in itself; and I felt certain also that his Oxford residence contributed essentially to the formation of his character in after-life. My doubts remain, but I have not thought them important enough to prevent my endeavoring at least to comply with her request; nor will I deny that I promise myself much pleasure, melancholy though it may be, in this attempt to recall those days. They had their troubles, I dare say; but in retrospect they always appear to me among the brightest and least checkered, if not the most useful, which have ever been vouchsafed to me.

Arnold and I, as you know, were undergraduates of Corpus Christi, a college very small in its numbers, and humble in its buildings, but to which we and our fellow-students formed an attachment never weakened in the after-course of our lives. At the time I speak of, 1809. and thenceforward for some few years, it was under the presidency, mild and inert, rather than paternal, of Dr. Cooke. His nephew, Dr. Williams, was the vice-president and medical fellow, the only lay-fellow permitted by the statutes. Retired he was in his habits, and not forward to interfere with the pursuits or studies of the young men. But I am bound to record, not only his learning and good taste, but the kindness of his heart, and his readiness to assist them by advice and criticism in their compositions. When I wrote for the Latin-verse prize in 1810, I was much indebted to him for advice in matters of taste and Latinity, and for the pointing out many faults in my rough verses.

Our tutors were the present Sedleian professor, the Rev. G. L. Cooke, and the lately deceased president, the Rev. T. Bridges. Of the former, because he is alive, I will only say that I believe no one ever attended his lectures without learning to admire his unwearied industry, patience, and good temper, and that few, if any, quitted his pupil-room without retaining a kindly feeling towards him. The recent death of Dr. Bridges would have affected Arnold as it has me. He was a most amiable man. The affectionate earnestness of his manner, and his high tone of feeling, fitted him especially to deal with young men. He made us always desirous of pleasing him: perhaps his fault was that he was too easily pleased. I am sure that he will be long and deeply regretted in the university

It was not, however, so much by the authorities of the college that Arnold's character was affected, as by its constitution and system, and by the residents whom it was his fortune to associate with familiarly there. I shall hardly do justice to my subject unless I state a few particulars as to the former, and what I am at liberty to mention as to the latter. Corpus is a very small establishment: twenty fellows and twenty scholars, with four exhibitioners, form the foundation. No independent members were admitted, except gentlemen commoners; and they were limited to six. Of the scholars, several were bachelors; and the whole number of students actually under college tuition seldom exceeded twenty. But the scholarships, though not entirely open, were yet enough so to admit of much competition; their value, and, still more, the creditable strictness and impartiality with which the examinations were conducted (qualities at that time more rare in college elections than now), insured a number of good candidates for each vacancy: and we boasted a more than proportionate share of successful competitors for university honors. It had been generally understood (I know not whether the statutes prescribe the practice), that, in the examinations, a large allowance was made for youth. Certain it was, that we had many very young candidates, and that, of these, many remarkable for early proficiency succeeded. We were then a small society, the members rather under the usual age, and with more than the ordinary proportion of ability and scholarship. Our mode of tuition was in harmony with these circumstances, not by private lectures, but in classes of such a size as excited emulation, and made us careful in the exact and neat rendering of the original, yet not so numerous as to prevent individual attention on the tutor's part, and familiar knowledge of each pupil's turn and talents. In addition to the books read in lecture, the tutor at the beginning of the term settled with each student upon some book to be read by himself in private, and prepared for the public examination at the end of term in Hall; and with this book, something on paper, either an analysis of it, or remarks upon it, was expected to be produced, which insured that the book should really have been read. It has often struck me since, that this whole plan, which is now, I believe, in common use in the university, was well devised for the tuition of young men of our age. We were not entirely set free from the leading-strings of the school: accuracy was cared for. We were accustomed to *vivâ voce* rendering, and *vivâ voce* question and answer in our lecture-room, before an audience of fellow-students whom we sufficiently respected. At the same time, the additional reading, trusted to ourselves alone, prepared us for accurate private study, and for our final exhibition in the schools.

One result of all these circumstances was, that we lived on the most familiar terms with each other. We might be, indeed we were, somewhat boyish in manner, and in the liberties we took with each other: but our interest in literature, ancient and modern, and in all the stirring matters of that stirring time, was not boyish; we debated the classic and romantic question; we discussed poetry and history, logic and philosophy; or we fought over the Peninsular battles and the Continental campaigns with the energy of disputants personally concerned in them. Our habits were inexpensive and temperate. One break-up party was held in the junior common room at the end of each term, in which we indulged our genius more freely, and our merriment, to say the truth, was somewhat exuberant and noisy; but the authorities wisely forbore too strict an inquiry into this.

It was one of the happy peculiarities of Corpus, that the bachelor scholars were compelled to residence. This regulation, seemingly inconvenient, but most wholesome, as I cannot but think for themselves, and now unwisely relaxed, operated very beneficially on the undergraduates; with the best and the most advanced of these, they associated very usefully: I speak here with grateful and affectionate remembrances of the privileges which I enjoyed in this way.

You will see that a society thus circumstanced was exactly one most likely to influence strongly the character of such a lad as Arnold was at his election. He came to us in Lent Term, 1811, from Winchester, winning his election against several very respectable candidates. He was a mere boy in appearance as well as in age, but we saw in a very short time that he was quite equal to take his part in the arguments of the common room; and he was, I rather think, admitted by Mr. Cooke at once into his senior class. As he was equal, so was he ready, to take part in our discussions: he was fond of conversation on serious matters, and vehement in argument; fearless, too, in advancing his opinions, which, to say the truth, often startled us a good deal; but he was ingenuous and candid; and though the fearlessness with which, so young as he was, he advanced his opinions might have seemed to betoken presumption, yet the good temper with which he bore retort or rebuke relieved him from that imputation; he was bold and warm, because, so far as his knowledge went, he saw very clearly, and he was an ardent lover of truth; but I never saw in him even then a grain of vanity or conceit. I have said that some of his opinions startled us a good deal: we were indeed, for the most part, Tories in Church and State, great respecters of things as they were, and not very tolerant of the disposition which he brought with him to question their wisdom. Many and long were the conflicts we had, and with unequal numbers. I think I have seen all the leaders of the common room engaged with him at once, with little order or consideration, as may be supposed, and not always with great scrupulosity as to the fairness of our arguments. This was attended by no loss of regard, and scarcely ever, or seldom, by even momentary loss of temper. We did not always convince him, — perhaps we ought not always to have done so, — yet in the end a considerable modification of his opinions was produced: in one of his letters to me, written at a much later period, he mentions this change. In truth, there were those among us calculated to produce an impression on his affectionate heart and ardent, ingenuous mind; and the rather, because the more we saw of him, and the more we' battled with him, the more manifestly did we respect and love him. The feeling with which we argued gave additional power to our arguments over a disposition such as his, and thus he became attached to young men of the most different tastes and intellects; his love for each taking a different color, more or less blended with respect, fondness, or even humor, according to those differences; and in return they all uniting in love and respect for him.

There will be some few to whom these remembrances will speak with touching truth: they will remember his single-hearted and devout schoolfellow, who early gave up his native land, and devoted himself to the missionary cause in India; the high-souled and imaginative, though somewhat indolent, lad, who came to us from Westminster; one bachelor, whose

father's connection with the House of Commons and residence
in Palace Yard made him a great authority with us as to the
world without, and the statesmen whose speeches he sometimes
heard, but we discussed much as if they had been personages
in history, and whose remarkable love for historical and geographical research, and his proficiency in it, with his clear
judgment, quiet humor, and mildness in communicating information, made him peculiarly attractive to Arnold; and, above
all, our senior among the undergraduates, though my junior
in years, the author of the " Christian Year," who came fresh
from the single teaching of his venerable father, and achieved
the highest honors of the university at an age when others
frequently are but on her threshold. Arnold clung to all these
with equal fidelity, but regarded each with different feelings :
each produced on him a salutary but different effect. His love
for all without exception, I know, if I know any thing of another man's heart, continued to his life's end : it survived (how
can the mournful facts be concealed in any complete and truth-
telling narrative of his life?) separation, suspension of intercourse, and entire disagreement of opinion, with the last of
these, on points believed by them both to be of essential
importance. These two held their opinions with a zeal and
tenacity proportionate to their importance : each believed the
other in error pernicious to the faith, and dangerous to himself :
and what they believed sincerely, each thought himself bound
to state, and stated it openly, it may be with too much of
warmth ; and unguarded expressions were unnecessarily, I think
inaccurately, reported. Such disagreements in opinion between
the wise and good are incident to our imperfect state ; and
even the good qualities of the heart, earnestness, want of suspicion, may lay us open to them : but, in the case before me,
the affectionate interest with which each regarded the other
never ceased. I had the good fortune to retain the intimate
friendship and correspondence of both; and I can testify with
authority, that the elder spoke and wrote of the younger as an
elder brother might of a younger, whom he tenderly loved,

though he disapproved of his course: while it was not in Arnold's nature to forget how much he had owed to Keble; he bitterly lamented, what he labored to avert, the suspension of their intimate intercourse: he was at all times anxious to renew it; and although, where the disagreement turned on points so vital between men who held each to his own so conscientiously, this may have been too much to expect, yet it is a most gratifying thought to their common friends, that they would probably have met at Fox How under Arnold's roof but a few weeks after he was called away to that state in which the doubts and controversies of this life will receive their clear resolution.

I return from my digression. Arnold came to us, of course, not a formed scholar, nor, I think, did he leave the college with scholarship proportioned to his great abilities and opportunities. And this arose, in part, from the decided preference which he gave to the philosophers and historians of antiquity over the poets, coupled with the distinction which he then made, erroneous as I think, and certainly extreme in degree, between words and things, as he termed it. His correspondence with me will show how much he modified this, too, in after-life; but at that time he was led by it to undervalue those niceties of language, the intimate acquaintance with which he did not then perceive to be absolutely necessary to a precise knowledge of the meaning of the author. His compositions, therefore, at this time, though full of matter, did not give promise of that clear and spirited style which he afterwards mastered: he gained no verse prize, but was an unsuccessful competitor for the Latin Verse in the year 1812, when Henry Latham succeeded, the third brother of that house who had done so; and though this is the only occasion on which I have any memorandum of his writing, I do not doubt that he made other attempts. Among us were several who were fond of writing English verse: Keble was even then raising among us those expectations which he has since so fully justified, and Arnold was not slow to follow the example. I have several poems of his written about this time, neat and pointed in expression, and just in thought, but not remarkable for fancy or imagination. I remember some years after, his telling me that he continued the practice "on principle:" he thought it a useful and humanizing exercise.

But, though not a poet himself, he was not insensible of the beauties of poetry, — far from it. I reflect with some pleasure, that I first introduced him to what has been somewhat unreasonably called the "Lake Poetry;" my near relation to one, and connection with another, of the poets, whose works were so called, were the occasion of this: and my uncle having sent me the "Lyrical Ballads," and the first edition of Mr. Wordsworth's poems, they became familiar among us. We were proof, I am glad to think, against the criticism, if so it might be called, of "The Edinburgh Review:" we felt their truth and beauty, and became zealous disciples of Wordsworth's philosophy. This was of peculiar advantage to Arnold, whose leaning was too direct for the practical and evidently useful: it brought out in him that feeling for the lofty and imaginative which appeared in all his intimate conversation, and may be seen spiritualizing those even of his writings in which, from their subject, it might seem to have less place. You know in later life how much he thought his beloved Fox How enhanced in value by its neighborhood to Rydal Mount, and what store he set on the privilege of frequent and friendly converse with the venerable genius of that sweet spot.

But his passion, at the time I am treating of, was for Aristotle and Thucydides: and however he became some few years after more sensible of the importance of the poets in classic literature, this passion he retained to the last; those who knew him intimately, or corresponded with him, will bear me witness how deeply he was imbued with the language and ideas of the former; how in earnest and unreserved conversation, or in writing, his train of thoughts was affected by the "Ethics" and "Rhetoric;" how he cited the maxims of the Stagirite as oracles, and how his language was quaintly and racily pointed with phrases from him. I never knew a man who made such familiar, even fond, use of an author; it is scarcely too much to say, that he spoke of him as of one intimately and affectionately known and valued by him; and when he was selecting his son's university, with much leaning for Cambridge, and many things which at the time made him incline against Oxford, dearly as he loved her, Aristotle turned the scale: "I could not consent," said he, "to send my son to a university where he would lose the study of him altogether." "You may believe," he said with regard to the London university, "that I have not forgotten the dear old Stagirite in our examinations; and I hope that he will be construed and discussed in Somerset House as well as in the schools." His fondness for Thucydides first prompted a Lexicon Thucydideum, in which he made some progress at Laleham in 1821 and 1822, and ended, as you know, in his valuable edition of that author.

Next to these he loved Herodotus. I have said that he was not, while I knew him at Oxford, a formed scholar, and that he composed stiffly and with difficulty; but to this there was a seeming exception: he had so imbued himself with the style of Herodotus and Thucydides, that he could write narratives in the style of either at pleasure with wonderful readiness, and, as we thought, with the greatest accuracy. I remember, too, an account by him of a "Vacation Tour in the Isle of Wight," after the manner of the "Anabasis."

Arnold's bodily recreations were walking and bathing. It was a particular delight to him, with two or three companions, to make what he called a skirmish across the country; on these occasions we deserted the road, crossed fences, and leaped ditches, or fell into them: he enjoyed the country round Oxford; and, while out in this way, his spirits would rise, and his mirth overflowed. Though delicate in appearance, and not giving promise of great muscular strength, yet his form was light, and he was capable of going long distances, and bearing much fatigue.

You know, that, to his last moment of health, he had the same predilections: indeed, he was, as much as any I ever knew, one whose days were

"Bound each to each by natural piety."

His manner had all the tastes and feelings of his youth, only more developed and better regulated. The same passion for the sea and shipping, and his favorite Isle of Wight; the same love for external nature, the same readiness in viewing the characteristic features of a country and its marked positions, or the most beautiful points of a prospect, for all which he was remarkable in after-life, — we noticed in him then. When Professor Buckland, then one of our fellows, began his career in that science, to the advancement of which he has contributed so much, Arnold became one of his most earnest and intelligent pupils; and you know how familiarly and practically he applied geological facts in all his later years.

In June, 1812, I was elected fellow of Exeter College, and determined to pursue the law as my profession: my residence at Oxford was thenceforward only occasional, but the friendship which had grown up between us suffered no diminution. Something, I forget now the particular circumstance, led to an interchange of letters, which ripened into a correspondence, continued with rather unusual regularity, when our respective occupations are considered, to within a few days of his death. It may show the opinion which I even then entertained of him, that I carefully preserved from the beginning every letter which I ever received from him: you have had an opportunity of judging of the value of the collection.

After I had ceased to reside, a small debating society, called the Attic Society, was formed in Oxford, which held its meetings in the rooms of the members by turns. Arnold was among the earliest members, and was, I believe, an embarrassed speaker. This I should have expected; for, however he might appear a confident advancer of his own opinions, he was, in truth, bashful, and at the same time had so acute a perception of what was ill-seasoned or irrelevant, that he would want that freedom from restraint which is essential at least to young speakers. This society was the germ of the Union, but I believe he never belonged to it.

In our days, the religious controversies had not begun, by which the minds of young men at Oxford are, I fear, now prematurely and too much occupied: the routine theological studies of the University were, I admit, deplorably low; but the earnest ones amongst us were diligent readers of Barrow, Hooker, and Taylor. Arnold was among these, but I have no recollection of any thing at that time distinctive in his religious opinions. What occurred afterwards does not properly fall within my chapter, yet it is not unconnected with it; and I believe I can sum up all that need be said on such a subject, as shortly and as accurately, from the sources of information in my hands, as any other person can. His was an anxiously inquisitive mind, a scrupulously conscientious heart: his inquiries, previously to his taking orders, led him on to distressing doubts on certain points in the Articles; these were not low nor rationalistic in their tendency, according to the bad sense of that term; there was no indisposition in him to believe merely because the article transcended his reason; he doubted the proof and the interpretation of the textual authority. His state was very painful, and I think morbid; for I remarked that the two occasions on which I was privy to his distress, were precisely those in which to doubt was against his dearest schemes of worldly happiness; and the consciousness of this seemed to make him distrustful of the arguments which were intended to lead his mind to acquiescence. Upon the first occasion to which I allude, he was a fellow of Oriel, and in close intercourse with one of the friends I have before mentioned, then also a fellow of the same college: to him as well as to me he opened his mind, and from him he received the wisest advice, which he had the wisdom to act upon; he was bid to pause in his inquiries, to pray earnestly for help and

light from above, and turn himself more strongly than ever to
the practical duties of a holy life : he did so, and through
severe trials was finally blessed with perfect peace of mind
and a settled conviction. If there be any so unwise as to
rejoice that Arnold, in his youth, had doubts on important doctrines, let him be sobered with the conclusion of those doubts,
when Arnold's mind had not become weaker, nor his pursuit
of truth less honest or ardent, but when his abilities were
matured, his knowledge greater, his judgment more sober : if
there be any who, in youth, are suffering the same distress
which befell him, let his conduct be their example, and the
blessing which was vouchsafed to him, their hope and consolation. In a letter from that friend to myself, of the date of Feb.
14, 1819, I find the following extract, which gives so true and
so considerate an account of this passage in Arnold's life, that
you may be pleased to insert it.

"I have not talked with Arnold lately on the distressing
thoughts which he wrote to you about ; but I am fearful, from
his manner at times, that he has by no means got rid of them,
though I feel quite confident that all will be well in the end.
The subject of them is that most awful one, on which all *very*
inquisitive reasoning minds are, I believe, most liable to such
temptations, — I mean the doctrine of the blessed Trinity. Do
not start, my dear Coleridge : I do not believe that Arnold
has any serious scruples of the *understanding* about it ; but it
is a defect of his mind, that he cannot get rid of a certain feeling of objections — and particularly when, as he fancies, the
bias is so strong upon him to decide one way from interest : he
scruples doing what I advise him, which is, to put down the
objections by main force whenever they arise in his mind, fearful that in so doing he shall be violating his conscience for
maintenance' sake. I am still inclined to think with you, that
the wisest thing he could do would be to take John M. (a
young pupil whom I was desirous of placing under his care)
and a curacy somewhere or other, and cure himself, not by
physic, — i.e., reading and controversy, — but by diet and regi-

men; i.e., holy living. In the mean. time, what an excellent fellow he is! I do think that one might safely say, as some one did of some other, 'One had better have Arnold's doubts than most men's certainties.'"

I believe I have exhausted my recollections; and if I have accomplished as I ought, what I proposed to myself, it will be hardly necessary for me to sum up formally his character as an Oxford undergraduate. At the commencement a boy, and at the close retaining, not ungracefully, much of boyish spirits, frolic, and simplicity; in mind vigorous, active, clear-sighted, industrious, and daily accumulating and assimilating treasures of knowledge; not averse to poetry, but delighting rather in dialectics, philosophy, and history, with less of imaginative than reasoning power; in argument bold almost to presumption, and vehement; in temper easily roused to indignation, yet more easily appeased, and entirely free from bitterness; fired, indeed, by what he deemed ungenerous or unjust to others, rather than by any sense of personal wrong; somewhat too little deferential to authority; yet without any real inconsistency, loving what was good and great in antiquity the more ardently and reverently because it was ancient; a casual or unkind observer might have pronounced him somewhat too pugnacious in conversation, and too positive. I have given, I believe, the true explanation: scarcely any thing would have pained him more than to be convinced that he had been guilty of want of modesty, or of deference where it was justly due; no one thought these virtues of more sacred obligation. In heart, if I can speak with confidence of any of the friends of my youth, I can of his, that it was devout and pure, simple, sincere, affectionate, and faithful.

It is time that I should close: already, I fear, I have dwelt with something like an old man's prolixity on passages of my youth, forgetting that no one can take the same interest in them which I do myself; that deep personal interest must, however, be my excuse. Whoever sets a right value on the events of his life for good or for evil, will agree, that next in importance to the rectitude of his own course and the selection of his partner for life, and far beyond all the wealth or honors which may reward his labor, far even beyond the unspeakable gift of bodily health, are the friendships which he forms in youth. That is the season when natures soft and pliant grow together, each becoming part of the other, and colored by it: thus, to become one in heart with the good and generous and devout, is, by God's grace, to become, in measure, good and generous and devout. Arnold's friendship has been one of the many blessings of my life. I cherish the memory of it with mournful gratitude, and I cannot but dwell with lingering fondness on the scene and the period which first brought us together. Within the peaceful walls of Corpus I made friends, of whom all are spared me but Arnold; he has fallen asleep: but the bond there formed, which the lapse of years and our differing walks in life did not unloosen, and which strong opposition of opinions only rendered more intimate, though interrupted in time, I feel not to be broken, — may I venture, without unseasonable solemnity, to express the firm trust, that it will endure forever in eternity!

Believe me, my dear Stanley,

Very truly yours,

J. T. C.

CHAPTER II.

LIFE AT LALEHAM.

THE society of the Fellows of Oriel College then, as for some time afterwards, numbered amongst its members some of the most rising men in the university; and it is curious to observe the list, which, when the youthful scholar of Corpus was added to it, contained the names of Copleston, Davison, Whately, Keble, Hawkins, and Hampden, and, shortly after he left it, those of Newman and Pusey, the former of whom was elected into his vacant fellowship. Amongst the friends with whom he thus became acquainted for the first time, may chiefly be mentioned Dr. Hawkins, since Provost of Oriel, to whom in the last year of his life he dedicated his " Lectures on Modern History ; " and Dr. Whately, afterwards principal of St. Alban's Hall, and now archbishop of Dublin, towards whom his regard was enhanced by the domestic intercourse which was constantly interchanged in later years between their respective families, and to whose writings and conversations he took an early opportunity of expressing his obligations in the preface to his first

volume of Sermons, in speaking of the various points
on which the communication of his friend's views had
" extended or confirmed his own."   For the next four
years he remained at Oxford, taking private pupils,
and reading extensively in the Oxford libraries, an
advantage which he never ceased to remember grate-
fully himself, and to impress upon others, and of which
the immediate results remain in a great number of
MSS., both in the form of abstracts of other works,
and of original sketches on history and theology.
They are remarkable rather as proofs of industry than
of power ; and the style of all his compositions, both
at this time and for some years later, is cramped by a
stiffness and formality alien alike to the homeliness of
his first published works and the vigor of his later ones,
and strikingly recalling his favorite lines,

> " The old man clogs our earliest years,
>   And simple childhood comes the last."

But already, in the examination for the Oriel Fellow-
ships, Dr. Whately had pointed out to the other elect-
ors the great capability of " growth " which he believed
to be involved in the crudities of the youthful candidate's exercises, and which, even in points where he
was inferior to his competitors, indicated an approaching superiority.   And widely different as were his
juvenile compositions in many points from those of
his after-life, yet it is interesting to observe in them
the materials which those who knew the pressure of
his numerous avocations used to wonder when he

could have acquired, and to trace amidst the strangest contrast of his general thoughts and style occasional remarks of a higher strain, which are in striking, though in some instances perhaps accidental, coincidence with some of his later views. He endeavored in his historical reading to follow the plan, which he afterwards recommended in his "Lectures," of making himself thoroughly master of some one period, — the fifteenth century, with "Philip de Comines" as his text-book, seems to have been the chief sphere of his studies, — and the first book after his election which appears in the Oriel Library as taken out in his name, is "Rymer's Fœdera." Many of the judgments of his maturer years on Gibbon, Livy, and Thucydides are to be found in a MS. of 1815, in which, under the name of "Thoughts on History," he went through the characteristics of the chief ancient and modern historians. And it is almost startling, in the midst of a rhetorical burst of his youthful Toryism in a journal of 1815, to meet with expressions of real feeling about the social state of England such as might have been written in his latest years; or amidst the commonplace remarks which accompany an analysis of St. Paul's Epistles and Chrysostom's "Homilies," in 1818, to stumble on a statement, complete as far as it goes, of his subsequent doctrine of the identity of Church and State.

Meanwhile he had been gradually led to fix upon his future course in life. In December, 1818, he was ordained deacon at Oxford: and on Aug. 11, 1820, he married Mary, youngest daughter of the Rev. John Penrose, rector of Fledborough, in Nottinghamshire, and sister of one of his earliest school and college friends, Trevenen Penrose ; having previously settled in 1819, at Laleham, near Staines, with his mother. aunt, and sister, where he remained for the next nine years, taking seven or eight young men as private pupils in preparation for the universities, for a short time in a joint establishment with his brother-in-law, Mr. Buckland, and afterwards independently by himself.

In the interval which had elapsed between the end of his undergraduate career at Oxford, and his entrance upon life, had taken place the great change from boyhood to manhood, and with it a corresponding change or growth of character, more marked and more important than at any subsequent period of his life. There was indeed another great step to be taken before his mind reached that later stage of development which was coincident with his transition from Laleham to Rugby. The prosaic and matter-of-fact element which has been described in his early Oxford life still retained its predominance, and to a certain extent dwarfed and narrowed his sphere of thought ; the various principles of political and theological science which contained in germ all that was to grow out of them, had not yet assumed their proper harmony and proportions ; his feelings of veneration, if less confined than in later years, were also less intense ; his hopes and views, if more practicable and more easily restrained by the advice of others, were also less wide in their range, and less lofty in their conception.

But, however great were the modifications which his character subsequently underwent, it is the change of tone at this time, between the earlier letters of this period (such as the one or two first of the ensuing series) and those which immediately succeed them, that marks the difference between the high spirit and warm feelings of his youth and the fixed earnestness and devotion which henceforth took possession of his whole heart and will. Whatever may have been the outward circumstances which contributed to this, — the choice of a profession, the impression left upon him by the sudden loss of his elder brother, the new and to him elevating influences of married life, the responsibility of having to act as the guide and teacher of others, — it was now for the first time that the principles, which before he had followed rather as a matter of course, and as held and taught by those around him, became emphatically part of his own convictions, to be embraced and carried out for life and for death.

From this time forward, such defects as were peculiar to his boyhood and early youth entirely disappear : the indolent habits ; the morbid restlessness and occasional weariness of duty ; the indulgence of vague schemes without definite purpose ; the intellectual doubts which beset the first opening of his mind to the realities of religious belief, when he shared, at least in part, the state of perplexity which in his later sermons he feelingly describes as the severest of earthly

trials, and which so endeared to him throughout life
the story of the confession of the apostle Thomas, —
all seem to have vanished away, and never again to
have diverted him from the decisive choice and ener-
getic pursuit of what he set before him as his end and
duty. From this time forward, no careful observer
can fail to trace that deep consciousness of the invisible world, and that power of bringing it before him in
the midst and through the means of his most active
engagements, which constituted the peculiarity of his
religious life, and the moving spring of his whole life.
It was not that he frequently introduced sacred names
in writing or in conversation, or that he often dwelt
on divine interpositions ; where many would have done
so without scruple, he would shrink from it : and in
speaking of his own religious feelings, or in appealing
to the religious feelings of others, he was, except to
those most intimate with him, exceedingly reserved. ¹
But what was true generally of the thorough interpene-
tration of the several parts of his character, was peculiarly true of it in its religious aspect : his natural
faculties were not unclothed, but clothed upon ; they
were at once colored by, and gave a color to, the belief which they received. It was in his common acts
of life, whether public or private, that the depth of his
religious convictions most visibly appeared : it was in
his manner of dwelling on religious subjects, that the
characteristic tendencies of his mind chiefly displayed
themselves.

Accordingly, whilst it is impossible, for this reason,

to understand his religious belief except through the knowledge of his actual life, and his writings on ordinary subjects, it is impossible, on the other hand, to understand his life and writings without bearing in mind how vivid was his realization of those truths of the Christian Revelation on which he most habitually dwelt. It was this which enabled him to undertake labors which, without such a power, must have crushed or enfeebled the spiritual growth which in him they seemed only to foster. It was the keen sense of thankfulness consciously awakened by every distinct instance of his many blessings, which more than any thing else explained his close union of joyousness with seriousness. In his even tenor of life, it was difficult for any one who knew him not to imagine " the golden chain of heavenward thoughts and humble prayers by which, whether standing or sitting, in the intervals of work or of amusement," he "linked together" his "more special and solemn devotions" (Sermons, vol. iii. p. 277) ; or not to trace something of the consciousness of an invisible presence in the collectedness with which, at the call of his common duties, he rose at once from his various occupations ; or in the calm repose which, in the midst of his most active labors, took all the disturbing accidents of life as a matter of course, and made toil so real a pleasure, and relaxation so real a refreshment, to him. And in his solemn and emphatic expressions on subjects expressly religious ; in his manner of awful reverence when speaking of God or of the Scriptures ; in his power of realizing the operation of something more than human, whether in his abhorrence of evil, or in his admiration of goodness, — the impression on those who heard him was often as though he knew what others only believed, as though he had seen what others only talked about. "No one could know him even a little," says one who was himself not amongst his most intimate friends, "and not be struck by his absolute wrestling with evil, so that like St. Paul he seemed to be battling with the wicked One, and yet with the feeling of God's help on his side, scorning as well as hating him."

Above all, it was necessary for a right understanding, not only of his religious opinions, but of his whole character, to enter into the peculiar feeling of love and adoration which he entertained towards our Lord Jesus Christ, — peculiar in the distinctness and intensity which, as it characterized almost all his common impressions, so in this case gave additional strength and meaning to those feelings with which he regarded not only his work of redemption, but himself as a living Friend and Master. "In that unknown world in which our thoughts become instantly lost," it was his real support and delight to remember that, "still there is one object on which our thoughts and imaginations may fasten, no less than our affections; that amidst the light, dark from excess of brilliance, which surrounds the throne of God, we may yet discern the gracious form of the Son of man." (Sermons, vol. iii. p. 90.) In that consciousness, which pressed upon him at times even heavily, of the difficulty of consider-

ing God in his own nature, believing, as he did, that
" Providence, the Supreme Being, the Deity, and other
such terms, repel us to an infinite distance," and that
the revelation of the Father, in himself unapproach-
able, is to be looked upon rather as the promise of
another life than as the support of this life, it was to
him a thought of perhaps more than usual comfort
to feel that " our God " is " Jesus Christ our Lord, the
image of the invisible God," and that " in him is rep-
resented all the fulness of the Godhead, until we know
even as we are known."   (Vol. v. p. 222.)   And with
this full conviction, both of his conscience and understanding, that he of whom he spoke was " still the
very selfsame Jesus in all human affections and divine
excellences," there was a vividness and tenderness in
his conception of him, on which, if one may so say,
all his feelings of human friendship and affection
seemed to fasten as on their natural object, " bringing
before him his actions, imaging to himself his very
voice and look," — there was to him (so to speak) a
greatness in the image thus formed of him, on which
all his natural instincts of reverence, all his range of
historical interest, all his admiration of truth and goodness, at once centred.   "Where can we find a name
so holy as that we may surrender our whole souls to
it, before which obedience, reverence without measure,
intense humility, most unreserved adoration, may all
be duly rendered?" was the earnest inquiry of his
whole nature, intellectual and moral, no less than religious.   And the answer to it in like manner expressed

what he endeavored to make the rule of his own personal conduct, and the centre of all his moral and religious convictions : " One name there is, and one alone, one alone in heaven and earth, — not truth, not justice, not benevolence, not Christ's mother, not his holiest servants, not his blessed sacraments, nor his very mystical body the Church, but himself only who died for us, and rose again, Jesus Christ, both God and man. (Sermons, vol. iv. p. 210.)

These were the feelings which, though more fully developed with the advance of years, now for the first time took thorough possession of his mind, and which struck upon his moral nature at this period with the same kind of force (if one may use the comparison) as the new views, which he acquired from time to time of persons and principles in historical or philosophical speculations, impressed themselves upon his intellectual nature. There is naturally but little to interrupt the retirement of his life at Laleham, which was only broken by the short tours in England or on the Continent, in which then, as afterwards, he employed his vacations. Still, it is not without interest to dwell on these years, the profound peace of which is contrasted so strongly with the almost incessant agitations of his subsequent life, and " to remain a while " (thus applying his own words on another subject) " on the high ground where the waters which are hereafter to form the separate streams " of his various social and theological views, " lie as yet undistinguished in their common parent lake."

Whatever may have been the exact notions of his future course which presented themselves to him, it is evident that he was not insensible to the attraction of visions of extensive influence ; and almost to his latest hour he seems to have been conscious of the existence of the temptation within him, and of the necessity of contending against it. " I believe," he said, many years afterwards, in speaking of these early struggles to a Rugby pupil who was consulting him on the choice of a profession,—" I believe that naturally I am one of the most ambitious men alive ;" and " the three great objects of human ambition," he added, to which alone he could look as deserving the name, were " to be the prime minister of a great kingdom, the governor of a great empire, or the writer of works which should live in every age and in every country." But in some respects the loftiness of his aims made it a matter of less difficulty to confine himself at once to a sphere in which, whilst he felt himself well and usefully employed, he felt also that the practical business of his daily duties acted as a check upon his own inclinations and speculations. Accordingly, when he entered upon his work at Laleham, he seems to have regarded it as his work for life. " I have always thought," he writes in 1823, " with regard to ambition, that I should like to be *aut Cæsar aut nullus ;* and, as it is pretty well settled for me that I shall not be Cæsar, I am quite content to live in peace as *nullus.*"

It was a period, indeed, on which he used himself to look back, even from the wider usefulness of his later years, almost with a fond regret, as to the happiest time of his life. " Seek ye first the kingdom of God and his righteousness, and then all other things shall be added to you," was a passage to which now more than any other time he was in the habit of recurring as one of peculiar truth and comfort. His situation supplied him exactly with that union of retirement and work which more than any other condition suited his natural inclinations, and enabled him to keep up more uninterrupted than was ever again in his power the communication which he so much cherished with his friends and relations. Without undertaking any directly parochial charge, he was in the habit of rendering constant assistance to Mr. Hearn, the curate of the place, both in the parish church and workhouse, and in visiting the villagers ; thus uniting with his ordinary occupations greater means than he was afterwards able to command, of familiar intercourse with his poorer neighbors, which he always so highly valued. Bound as he was to Laleham by all these ties, he long loved to look upon it as his final home ; and the first reception of the tidings of his election at Rugby was overclouded with deep sorrow at leaving the scene of so much happiness. Years after he had left it, he still retained his early affection for it ; and till he had purchased his house in Westmoreland, he entertained a lingering hope that he might return to it in his old age, when he should have retired from Rugby. Often he would revisit it, and delighted in renewing his acquaintance with all the families of the poor whom he had known during his residence, in showing to his children his former haunts, in looking once again on his favorite views of the great plain of Middlesex; the lonely walks along the quiet banks of the Thames; the retired garden, with its "Campus Martius" and its "wilderness of trees," which lay behind his house, and which had been the scenes of so many sportive games and serious conversations; the churchyard of Laleham, then doubly dear to him as containing the graves of his infant child whom he buried there in 1832, and of his mother, his aunt, and his sister Susannah, who had long formed almost a part of his own domestic circle, and whom he lost within a few years after his departure to Rugby.

His general view of his work as a private tutor is best given in his own words in 1831, to a friend who was about to engage in a similar occupation.

"I know it has a bad name, but my wife and I always happened to be fond of it; and if I were to leave Rugby for no demerit of my own, I would take to it again with all the pleasure in life. I enjoyed, and do enjoy, the society of youths of seventeen or eighteen, for they are all alive in limbs and spirits at least, if not in mind; while in older persons the body and spirits often become lazy and languid, without the mind gaining any vigor to compensate for it. Do not take your work as a dose, and I do not think you will find it nauseous. I am sure you will not if your wife does not; and, if she is a sensible woman, she will not either if you do not. The misery of private tuition seems to me to consist in this, that men enter upon it as a means to some further end; are always impatient for the time when they may lay it aside: whereas if you enter upon it heartily as your life's business, as a man enters upon any other profession, you are not then in danger of grudging every hour you give to it, and thinking of how much privacy and how much society it is robbing you; but you take to it as a matter of course, making it your material occupation, and devote your time to it, and then you find that it is in itself full of interest, and keeps life's current fresh and wholesome by bringing you in such perpetual contact with all the spring of youthful liveliness. I should say, have your pupils a good deal with you, and be as familiar with them as you possibly can. I did this continually more and more before I left Laleham, going to bathe with them, leaping, and all other gymnastic exercises within my capacity, and sometimes sailing or rowing with them. They, I believe, always liked it; and I enjoyed it myself like a boy, and found myself constantly the better for it."

In many respects, his method at Laleham resembled the plan which he pursued on a larger scale at Rugby. Then, as afterwards, he had a strong sense of the duty of protecting his charge, at whatever risk to himself, from the presence of companions who were capable only of exercising an evil influence over their associates; and, young as he was, he persisted in carrying out this principle, and in declining to take any additional pupils as long as he had under him any of such a character, whom yet he did not feel himself justified in removing at once. And in answer to the request of his friends that he would raise his terms, " I am confirmed in my resolution not to do so," he writes in 1827, " lest I should get the sons of very great people as my pupils whom it is almost impossible to *sophronize*." In reply to a friend in 1821, who had asked his advice in a difficult case of dealing with a pupil, —

"I have no doubt," he answers, "that you have acted perfectly right: for lenity is seldom to be repented of; and besides, if you should find that it has been ill bestowed, you can have recourse to expulsion after all. But it is clearly right to try your chance of making an impression; and, if you can make any at all, it is at once your justification and encouragement to proceed. It is very often like kicking a football up-hill: you kick it onwards twenty yards, and it rolls back nineteen; still, you have gained one yard, and thus in a good many kicks you make some progress. This, however, is on the supposition that the pupil's fault is ακρασια and not κακια: for if he laughs behind your back at what you say to him, he will corrupt others; and then there is no help for it, but he must go. This is to me all the difference: I would be as patient as I possibly could with irresolution, unsteadiness, and fits of idleness: but if a pupil has set his mind to do nothing, but considers all the work as so much fudge, which he will evade if he can, I have made up my resolution that I will send him away without scruple; for not to speak of the heartless trouble that such an animal would give to myself, he is a living principle of mischief in the house, being ready at all times to pervert his companions: and this determination I have expressed publicly, and if I know myself I will act upon it, and I advise you most heartily to do the same. Thus, then, with Mr. ——, when he appeared penitent, and made professions of amendment, you were clearly right to give him a longer trial. If he be sincere, however unsteady and backsliding, he will not hurt the principles of your other pupils; for he will not glory in his own misconduct, which I suppose is the danger: but if you have reason to think that the impression you made on him was only temporary, and that it has since entirely gone away, and his own evil principles as well as evil practices are in vigor, then I would advise you to send him off without delay; for then, taking the mischief he will do to others into the account, the football rolls down twenty-five yards to your kick of twenty, and that is a losing game."

"'Εχθιστη ὀδύνη πολλὰ φρονέοντα πὲρ μηδένος κρατέειν," he writes, "must be the feelings of many a working tutor who cannot open the eyes of his pupils to see what knowledge is, — I do not mean human knowledge only, but 'wisdom.'"

"You could scarcely conceive the rare instances of ignorance that I have met with amongst them. One had no notion of what was meant by an angle; another could not tell how many Gospels there are, nor could he, after mature deliberation, recollect any other names than Matthew, Mark, and Luke; and a third holds the first concord in utter contempt, and makes the infinitive mood supply the place of the principal verb in the sentence without the least suspicion of any impropriety. My labor, therefore, is more irksome than I have ever known it; but none of my pupils give me any uneasiness on the most serious points, and five of them staid the sacrament when it was last administered. I ought constantly to impress upon my mind how light an evil is the greatest ignorance or dulness when compared with habits of profligacy, or even of wilful irregularity and riotousness."

"I regret in your son," he says (in writing to a parent), "a carelessness which does not allow him to think seriously of what he is living for, and to do what is right, not merely as a matter of regularity, but because it is a duty. I trust you will not think that I am meaning any thing more than my words convey, or that what I am regretting in your son is not to be found in nineteen out of every twenty young men of his age; but I conceive that you would wish me to form my desire of what your son should be, not according to the common standard, but according to the highest, — to be satisfied with no less in him than I should have been anxious to find in a son of my own. He is capable of doing a great deal, and I have not seen any thing in him which has called for reproof since he has been with me. I am only desirous that he should work more heartily, — just, in short, as he would work if he took an interest of himself in his own improvement. On this, of course, all distinction in Oxford must depend: but much more than distinction depends on it; for the difference between a useful education, and one which does not affect the future life, rests mainly on the greater or less activity which it has communicated to the pupil's mind, whether he has learned to think, or to act, and to gain knowledge by himself, or whether he has merely followed passively as long as there was some one to draw him.''

It is needless to anticipate the far more extended influence which he exercised over his Rugby scholars, by describing in detail the impression produced upon his pupils at Laleham. Yet the mere difference of the relation in which he stood towards them in itself gave a peculiar character to his earlier sphere of education, and as such may best be described in the words of one amongst those whom he most esteemed, Mr. Price, who afterwards became one of his assistant masters at Rugby.

" Nearly eighteen years have passed away since I resided at Laleham, and I had the misfortune of being but two months as a pupil there. I am unable, therefore, to give you a complete picture of the Laleham life of my late revered tutor: I can only impart to you such impressions as my brief sojourn there has indelibly fixed in my recollection.

" The most remarkable thing which struck me at once on joining the Laleham circle was the wonderful healthiness of tone and feeling which prevailed in it. Every thing about me I immediately found to be most real : it was a place where a new-comer at once felt that a great and earnest work was going forward. Dr. Arnold's great power as a private tutor resided in this, that he gave such an intense earnestness to life. Every pupil was made to feel that there was a work for him to do, — that his happiness as well as his duty lay in doing that work well. Hence, an indescribable zest was communicated to a young man's feeling about life; a strange joy came over him on discovering that he had the means of being useful, and thus of being happy; and a deep respect and ardent attachment sprang up towards him who had taught him thus to value life and his own self, and his work and mission in this world. All this was founded on the breadth and comprehensiveness of Arnold's character, as well as its striking truth and reality; on the unfeigned regard he had for work of all kinds, and the sense he had of its value, both for the complex aggregate of society, and the growth and perfection of the individual. Thus pupils of the most different natures were keenly stimulated: none felt that he was left out, or that, because he was not endowed with large powers of mind, there was no sphere open to him in the honorable pursuit of usefulness. This wonderful power of making all his pupils respect themselves, and of awakening in them a consciousness of the duties that God had assigned to them personally, and of the consequent reward each should have of his labors, was one of Arnold's most characteristic features as a trainer of youth; he possessed it eminently at Rugby; but, if I may trust my own vivid recollections, he had it quite as remarkably at Laleham. His hold over all his pupils I know perfectly astonished me. It was not so much an enthusiastic admiration for genius or learning or eloquence which stirred within them: it was a sympathetic thrill, caught from a spirit that was earnestly at work in the world — whose work was healthy, sustained, and constantly carried forward in the fear of God — a work that was founded on a deep sense of its duty and its value, and was coupled with such a true humility, such an unaffected simplicity, that others could not help being invigorated by the same feeling, and with the belief that they, too, in their measure, could go and do likewise.

" In all this there was no excitement, no predilection for one class of work above another, no enthusiasm for any one-sided object, but an humble, profound, and most religious consciousness, that work is the appointed calling of man on earth, the end for which his various faculties were given, the element in which his nature is ordained to develop itself, and in which his progressive advance towards heaven is to lie. Hence, each pupil felt assured of Arnold's sympathy in his own particular growth and character of talent : in striving to cultivate his own gifts, in whatever direction they might lead him, he infallibly found Arnold not only approving, but positively and sincerely valuing for themselves, the results he had arrived at; and that approbation and esteem gave a dignity and a worth, both to himself and his labor.

" His humility was very deeply seated; his respect for all knowledge sincere. A strange feeling passed over the pupil's mind when he found great and often undue credit given him for knowledge of which his tutor was ignorant. But this generated no conceit : the example before his eyes daily reminded him that it was only as a means of usefulness, as an improvement of talents for his own good and that of others, that knowledge was valued. He could not find comfort in the presence of such reality, in any shallow knowledge.

" There was then, as afterwards, great simplicity in his religious character. It was no isolated part of his nature, it was a bright and genial light shining on every branch of his life. He took very great pains with the Divinity lessons of his pupils; and his lectures were admirable, and, I distinctly remember, very highly prized for their depth and originality. Neither generally in ordinary conversation, nor in his walks with his pupils, was his style of speaking directly or mainly religious; but he was ever very ready to discuss any religious question : whilst the depth and truth of his nature, and the earnestness of his religious convictions and feelings, were ever bursting forth, so as to make it strongly felt that his life, both outward and inward, was rooted in God.

" In the details of daily business, the quantity of time that he devoted to his pupils was very remarkable. Lessons began at seven, and with the interval of breakfast lasted till nearly three: then he would walk with his pupils, and dine at half-past five. At seven he usually had some lesson on hand; and it was only when we all were gathered up in the drawing-room after tea, amidst young men on all sides of him, that he would commence work for himself, in writing his Sermons or Roman History.

"Who that ever had the happiness of being at Laleham, does not remember the lightness and joyousness of heart with which he would romp and play in the garden, or plunge with a boy's delight into the Thames, or the merry fun with which he would battle with spears with his pupils? Which of them does not recollect how the tutor entered into his amusements with scarcely less glee than himself?

"But I must conclude: I do not pretend to touch on every point. I have told you what struck me most, and I have tried to keep away all remembrance of what he was when I knew him better. I have confined myself to the impression Laleham left upon me.

"B. PRICE."

TO J. T. COLERIDGE, ESQ.

(In answer to criticisms on a review of Poppo's Observationes Criticæ.)

LALEHAM GARDEN, April 25, 1821.

. . . Now for your remarks on my Poppo. All clumsiness in the sentences, and want of connection between the parts, I will do my best to amend; and the censure on verbal criticism I will either soften or scratch out entirely, for J. Keble objected to the same part. The translations also I will try to improve, and indeed I am aware of their baldness. The additions which you propose, I can make readily: but as to the general plainness of the style, I do not think I clearly see the fault which you allude to; and, to say the truth, the plainness, i.e., the absence of ornament and long words, is the result of deliberate intention. At any rate, in my own case, I am sure an attempt at ornament would make my style so absurd that you would yourself laugh at it. I could not do it naturally; for I have now so habituated myself to that unambitious and plain way of writing, and absence of Latin words as much as possible, that I could not write otherwise without manifest affection. Of course I do not mean to justify awkwardness and clumsy sentences, of which I am afraid my writings are too full, and all which I will do my best to alter wherever you have marked them; but any thing like puff, or verbal ornament, I cannot bring myself to. Richness of style I admire heartily, but this I cannot attain to for lack of power. All I could do would be to produce a bad imitation of it, which seems to me very ridiculous. For the same reason, I know not how to make the review more striking: I cannot make it so by its own real weight and eloquence, and therefore I think I should only make it offensive by trying to make it fine. Do consider, what you recommend is ἁπλῶς ἄριστον, but I must do what is ἄριστον ἐμοί. You know you always told me I should never be a poet; and in like manner I never could be really eloquent, for I have not the imagination or fulness of mind needful to make me so. . . .

TO REV. E. HAWKINS.

LALEHAM, Oct. 21, 1827.

I feel most sincerely obliged to you and my other friends in Oxford for the kind interest which you show in my behalf, in wishing to procure for me the head mastership at Rugby. Of its being a great deal more lucrative than my present employment I have no doubt, nor of its being in itself a situation of more extensive usefulness; but I do doubt whether it would be so in my hands, and how far I am fitted for the place of head master of a large school. . . . I confess that I should very much object to undertake a charge in which I was not invested with pretty full discretion. According to my notions of what large schools are, founded on all I know, and all I have ever heard of them, expulsion should be practised much oftener than it is. Now, I know that trustees, in general, are averse to this plan, because it has a tendency to lessen the numbers of the school ; and they regard quantity more than quality. In fact, my opinions on this point might, perhaps, generally be considered as disqualifying me for the situation of master of a great school; yet I could not consent to tolerate much that I know is tolerated generally, and, therefore, I should not like to enter on an office which I could not discharge according to my own views of what is right. I do not believe myself, that my system would be, in fact, a cruel or a harsh one; and I believe, that, with much care on the part of the masters, it would be seldom necessary to proceed to the *ratio ultima:* only I would have it clearly understood, that I would must unscrupulously resort to it, at whatever inconvenience, where there was a perseverance in any habit inconsistent with a boy's duties.

TO REV. E. HAWKINS.

LALEHAM, Dec. 28, 1827.

Your kind little note ought not to have remained thus long unanswered, especially as you have a most particular claim on my thanks for your active kindness in the whole business, and for your character of me to Sir H. Halford, that I was likely to improve generally the system of public education, a statement which Sir H. Halford told me had weighed most strongly in my favor. You would not, I am sure, have recommended me, if you had supposed that I should alter things violently or for the pleasure of altering; but, as I have at different times expressed in conversation my disapprobation of much of the existing system, I find that some people expect that I am going to sweep away root and branch, *quod absit!* I need not tell you how wholly unexpected this result has been to us, and I hope I need not say also what a solemn and almost overwhelming responsibility I feel is imposed on me. I would hope to have the prayers of my friends, together with my own, for a supply of that true wisdom which is required for such a business. To be sure, how small in comparison is the importance of my teaching the boys to read Greek, and how light would be a schoolmaster's duty if that were all of it! Yet, if my health and strength continue as they have been for the last eight years, I do not fear the labor, and really enjoy the prospect of it. I am so glad that we are likely to meet soon in Oxford.

TO THE REV. JOHN TUCKER.

LALEHAM, August, 1828.

I am inclined to write to you once again before we leave Laleham, as a sort of farewell from this dear place ; and you shall answer it with a welcome to Rugby. You fancy us already at Rugby; and so does J. Keble, from whom I received a very kind letter some time since, directed to me there. But we do not move till Tuesday, when we go, fourteen souls, to Oxford, having taken the whole coach; and on Wednesday we hope to reach Rugby, having in like manner secured the whole Leicester coach from Oxford to Rugby. Our goods and chattels, under convoy of our gardener, are at this time somewhere on the Grand Junction Canal, and will reach Rugby, I hope, this evening. The poor house here is sadly desolate, — all the carpets up, half the furniture gone, and signs of removal everywhere visible. And so ends the first act of my life since I arrived at manhood. For the last eight years it has been a period of as unruffled happiness as I should think could ever be experienced by man. Mary's illness, in 1821, is almost its only dark spot; — and how was that softened and comforted! It is almost a fearful consideration; and yet there is a superstitious notion, and an unbelieving one too, which cannot receive God's mercies as his free gift, but will always be looking out for something wherewith to purchase them. An humbling consideration much rather it is and ought to be: yet all life is humbling, if we think upon it; and our greatest mercies, which we sometimes least think of, are the most humbling of all. . . . The Rugby prospect I contemplate with a very strong interest: the work I am not afraid of, if I can get my proper exercise; but I want absolute play, like a boy, and neither riding nor walking will make up for my leaping-pole and gallows, and bathing, when the youths used to go with me, and I felt completely for the time a boy, as they were. It is this entire relaxation, I think, at intervals, such again as my foreign tours have afforded, that gives me so keen an appetite for my work at other times, and has enabled me to go through it, not only with no fatigue, but with a sense of absolute pleasure. I believe that I am going to publish a volume of Sermons. You will think me crazed perhaps; but I have two reasons for it, — chiefly, the repeated exhortations of several individuals for the last three or four years; but these would not alone have urged me to it, did I not wish to state, for my own sake, what my opinions really are, on points where I know they have been grievously misrepresented. Whilst I lived here in Laleham, my opinions mattered to nobody: but I know, that, while I was a candidate for Rugby, it was said in Oxford that I did not preach the gospel, nor even touch upon the great doctrines of Christianity in my sermons; and, if this same impression be prevalent now, it will be mischievous to the school in a high degree. Now, if what I really do preach be to any man's notions not the gospel, I cannot help it, and must be content to abide by the consequences of his opinion; but I do not want to be misunderstood, and accused of omitting things which I do not omit.

TO THE REV. GEORGE CORNISH.

RUGBY, Aug. 16, 1828.

. . . If I can do my work as I ought to do it, we shall have every reason to be thankful for the change. I must not, it is true, think of dear old Laleham, and all that we have left there, or the perfect peace of our eight years of wedded life passed there together.   It is odd that both you and I should now for the first time in our lives be moving from our parents' neighborhood; but in this respect our happiness was very uncommon: and to me altogether, Laleham was so like a place of premature rest, that I believe I ought to be sincerely thankful that I am called to a scene of harder and more anxious labor. . . . The boys come back next Saturday week.   So here begins the second act of our lives.   May God bless it to us, and make it help forward the great end of all!

CHAPTER III.

SCHOOL LIFE AT RUGBY.

IT would be useless to give any chronological details of a life so necessarily monotonous as that of the head master of a public school, and it is accordingly only intended to describe the general system which Dr. Arnold pursued during the fourteen years he was at Rugby. Yet some apology may seem to be due for the length of a chapter which to the general reader must be comparatively deficient in interest. Something must, indeed, be forgiven to the natural inclination to dwell on those recollections of his life which to his pupils are the most lively and the most recent — something to the almost unconscious tendency to magnify those scenes which are most nearly connected with what is most endeared to one's self. But, independently of any local or personal considerations, it has been felt, that, if any part of Dr. Arnold's work deserved special mention, it was his work at Rugby; and that, if it was to be of any use to those of his own profession who would take any interest in it, it could only be made so by a full and minute account.

Those who look back upon the state of English education in the year 1827, must remember how the feeling of dissatisfaction with existing institutions which had begun in many quarters to display itself, had already directed considerable attention to the condition of public schools.   The range of classical reading, in itself confined, and with no admixture of other information, had been subject to vehement attacks from the liberal party generally, on the ground of its alleged narrowness and inutility.   And the more undoubted evil of the absence of systematic attempts to give a more directly Christian character to what constituted the education of the whole English gentry, was becoming more and more a scandal in the eyes of religious men, who at the close of the last century and the beginning of this, — Wilberforce, for example, and Bowdler, — had lifted up their voices against it.   A complete reformation, or a complete destruction of the whole system, seemed, to many persons, sooner or later to be inevitable.   The difficulty, however, of making the first step, where the alleged objection to alteration was its impracticability, was not to be easily surmounted.   The mere resistance to change which clings to old institutions, was in itself a considerable obstacle, and in the case of some of the public schools, from the nature of their constitution, in the first instance almost insuperable ; and whether amongst those who were engaged in the existing system, or those who were most vehemently opposed to it, for opposite but obvious reasons, it must have been extremely difficult to find a man who would attempt, or, if he attempted, carry through, any extensive improvement.

It was at this juncture that Dr. Arnold was elected head master of a school, which, whilst it presented a fair average specimen of the public schools at that time, yet by its constitution imposed fewer shackles on its head, and offered a more open field for alteration, than was the case at least with Eton or Winchester. The post itself, in spite of the publicity, and to a certain degree formality, which it entailed upon him, was in many respects remarkably suited to his natural tastes, — to his love of tuition, which had now grown so strongly upon him, that he declared sometimes that he could hardly live without such employment ; to the vigor and spirits which fitted him rather to deal with the young than the old ; to the desire of carrying out his favorite ideas, of uniting things secular with things spiritual, and of introducing the highest principles of action into regions comparatively uncongenial to their reception.

Even his general interest in public matters was not without its use in his new station. Many, indeed, both of his admirers and of his opponents, used to lament that a man with such views and pursuits should be placed in such a situation. "What a pity," it was said on the one hand, "that a man fit to be a statesman, should be employed in teaching school-boys." "What a shame," it was said on the other hand, "that the head master of Rugby should be employed in writing essays and pamphlets." But even had there been no connection between the two spheres of his interest, and had the inconvenience resulting from his public prominence been far greater than it was, it would have been the necessary price of having him at all in that place. He would not have been himself had he not felt and written as he did ; and he could not have endured to live under the grievance of remaining silent on subjects on which he believed it to be his most sacred duty to speak what he thought.

As it was, however, the one sphere played into the other. Whatever labor he bestowed on his literary works was only part of that constant progress of self-education which he thought essential to the right discharge of his duties as a teacher. Whatever interest he felt in the struggles of the political and ecclesiastical world re-acted on his interest in the school, and invested it in his eyes with a new importance. When he thought of the social evils of the country, it awakened a corresponding desire to check the thoughtless waste and selfishness of school-boys ; a corresponding sense of the aggravation of those evils by the insolence and want of sympathy too frequently shown by the children of the wealthier classes towards the lower orders ; a corresponding desire that they should there imbibe the first principles of reverence to law, and regard for the poor, which the spirit of the age seemed to him so little to encourage. When he thought of the evils of the Church, he would " turn from the thought of the general temple in ruins, and see whether they could not, within the walls of their own little particular congregation," endeavor to realize what he believed to be its true idea ; " what use they could make of the vestiges of it, still left amongst themselves, — common reading of the Scriptures, common prayer, and the communion." (Sermons, vol. iv. pp. 266, 316.) Thus, " whatever of striking good or evil happened in any part of the wide range of English dominion," — " declared on what important scenes some of his own scholars might be called upon to enter," — " whatever new and important things took place in the world of thought," suggested the hope " that they, when they went forth amidst the strifes of tongues and of minds, might be endowed with the spirit of wisdom and power." (Sermons, vol. v. p. 405.) And even in the details of the school, it would be curious to trace how he recognized in the peculiar vices of boys, the same evils which, when full grown, became the source of so much social mischief; how he governed the school precisely on the same principles as he would have governed a great empire ; how constantly, to his own mind or to his scholars, he exemplified the highest truths of theology and philosophy in the simplest relations of the boys towards each other or towards him.

In entering upon his office, he met with difficulties, many of which have since passed away, but which must be borne in mind if points are here dwelt upon that have now ceased to be important, but were by no means insignificant or obvious when he came to Rugby. Nor did his system at once attain its full maturity. He was a long time feeling his way amongst the various institutions which he formed or invented; he was con-

stantly striving after an ideal standard of perfection
which he was conscious that he had never attained;
to the improvements which, in a short time, began to
take place in other schools, — to those at Harrow,
under his friend Dr. Longley, and to those at Winchester, under Dr. Moberly, to which he alluded in
one of his later sermons (vol. v. p. 150), — he often
looked as models for himself; to suggestions from
persons very much younger than himself, not unfre-
quently from his former pupils, with regard to the
course of reading, or to alterations in his manner of
preaching, or to points of discipline, he would often
listen with the greatest deference.   His own mind was
constantly devising new measures for carrying out his
several views.   "The school," he said on first coming,
"is quite enough to employ any man's love of reform;
and it is much pleasanter to think of evils which you
may yourself hope to relieve, than those with regard
to which you can give nothing but vain wishes and
opinions."   "There is enough of Toryism in my nature," he said, on evils being mentioned to him in the
place, "to make me very apt to sleep contentedly over
things as they are : and therefore I hold it to be most
true kindness when any one directs my attention to
points in the school which are alleged to be going on
ill."

The perpetual succession of changes which resulted
from this, was by many objected to as excessive, and
calculated to endanger the stability of his whole system.   "He wakes every morning," it was said of him,

"with the impression that every thing is an open question." But, rapid as might be the alterations to which the details of his system were subjected, his general principles remained fixed. The unwillingness which he had, even in common life, to act in any individual case without some general law to which he might refer it, ran through every thing; and at times it would almost seem as if he invented universal rules with the express object of meeting particular cases. Still, if in smaller matters this gave an occasional impression of fancifulness or inconsistency, it was, in greater matters, one chief cause of the confidence which he inspired. Amidst all the plans that came before him, he felt, and he made others feel, that, whatever might be the merits of the particular question at issue, there were principles behind which lay far more deeply seated than any mere question of school government, which he was ready to carry through at whatever cost, and from which no argument or menace could move him.

Of the mere external administration of the school, little need here be said. Many difficulties which he encountered were alike provoked and subdued by the peculiarities of his own character. The vehemence with which he threw himself into a contest against evil, and the confidence with which he assailed it, though it carried him through perplexities to which a more cautious man would have yielded, led him to disregard interests and opinions which a less earnest or a less sanguine reformer would have treated with greater consideration. His consciousness of his own integrity, and his contempt for worldly advantage, sometimes led him to require from others more than might be reasonably expected from them, and to adopt measures which the world at large was sure to misinterpret; yet these very qualities, in proportion as they became more appreciated, ultimately secured for him a confidence beyond what could have been gained by the most deliberate circumspection. But, whatever were the temporary exasperations and excitements thus produced in his dealings with others, they were gradually removed by the increasing control over himself and his work which he acquired in later years. The readiness which he showed to acknowledge a fault when once convinced of it, as well as to persevere in kindness, even when he thought himself injured, succeeded in healing breaches which, with a less forgiving or less honest temper, would have been irreparable. His union of firmness with tenderness had the same effect in the settlement of some of the perplexities of his office which in others would have resulted from art and management; and even his work as a schoolmaster cannot be properly appreciated without remembering how, in the end of his career, he rallied round him the public feeling, which in its beginning and middle, as will appear farther on, had been so widely estranged from him.

With regard to the trustees of the school, entirely amicable as were his usual relations with them, and grateful as he felt to them for their active support and personal friendliness, he from the first maintained, that, in the actual working of the school, he must be completely independent, and that their remedy, if they were dissatisfied, was not interference, but dismissal. On this condition he took the post; and any attempt to control either his administration of the school, or his own private occupations, he felt bound to resist "as a duty," he said on one occasion, "not only to himself, but to the master of every foundation school in England."

Of his intercourse with the assistant masters it is for obvious reasons impossible to speak in any detail. Yet it would be injustice alike to them and to him, not to bear in mind how earnestly he dwelt on their co-operation as an essential part of his own government of the school. It was one of his main objects to increase in all possible ways their importance. By raising their salaries he obviated the necessity of their taking any parochial duty which should divert their attention from the school, and procured from the bishop of the diocese the acknowledgment of their situations as titles for orders. A system of weekly councils was established, in which all school-matters were discussed; and he seldom or never acted in any important point of school discipline without consulting them. It was his endeavor, partly by placing the boarding-houses under their care, partly by an elaborate system of private tuition, which was introduced with this express purpose, to encourage a pastoral and friendly relation between them and the several classes of boys intrusted to them. What he was in his department, in short,

he wished every one of them to be in theirs; and
nothing rejoiced him more than to hear of instances
in which he thought that boys were sent to the school
for the sake of his colleagues' instructions rather than
of his own.   It was his labor to inspire them with
the views of education and of life by which he was
possessed himself; and the bond thus gradually
formed, especially when in his later time several of
those who had been his pupils became his colleagues,
grew deeper and stronger with each successive year
that they passed in the place.   Out of his own family,
there was no circle of which he was so completely the
animating principle, as amongst those who co-operated
with him in the great practical work of his life; none
in which his loss was so keenly felt to be irreparable,
or his example so instinctively regarded in the light
of a living spring of action and a source of solemn
responsibility, as amongst those who were called to
continue their labors in the sphere and on the scene
which had been ennobled to them by his counsels and
his presence.[1]

[1] His views will perhaps be best explained by the two following letters: —

LETTER OF INQUIRY FOR A MASTER.

. . . "What I want is a man who is a Christian and a gentleman, an active
man, and one who has common sense, and understands boys. I do not so
much care about scholarship, as he will have immediately under him the lowest
forms in the school; but yet, on second thoughts, I do care about it very
much, because his pupils may be in the highest forms; and, besides, I think
that even the elements are best taught by a man who has a thorough knowledge of the matter. However, if one must give way, I prefer activity of mind
and an interest in his work to high scholarship; for the one may be acquired
far more easily than the other. I should wish it also to be understood, that the

But whatever interest attaches to the more external circumstances of his administration, and to his relations with others, who were concerned in it, is, of course, centred in his own personal government of the boys. The natural effect of his concentration of interest on what he used to call " our great self," the school, was that the separate existence of the school was in return almost merged in him. This was not indeed his own intention; but it was precisely because he thought so much of the institution, and so little of himself, that, in spite of his efforts to make it work independently of any personal influence of his own,

new master may be called upon to take boarders in his house; it being my intention for the future to require this of all masters as I see occasion, that so in time the boarding-houses may die a natural death. . . . With this to offer, I think I have a right to look rather high for the man whom I fix upon; and it is my great object to get here a society of intelligent, gentlemanly, and active men, who may permanently keep up the character of the school, and make it ' vile damnum,' if I were to break my neck to-morrow."

LETTER TO A MASTER ON HIS APPOINTMENT.

. . . " The qualifications which I deem essential to the due performance of a master's duties here may, in brief, be expressed as the spirit of a Christian and a gentleman, — that a man should enter his business, not ἐκ παρέργου, but as a substantive and most important duty; that he should devote himself to it as the especial branch of the ministerial calling which he has chosen to follow — that belonging to a great public institution, and standing in a public and conspicuous situation, he should study things ' lovely and of good report;' that is, that he should be public-spirited, liberal, and entering heartily into the interest, honor, and general respectability and distinction of the society which he has joined; and that he should have sufficient vigor of mind, and thirst for knowledge, to persist in adding to his own stores without neglecting the full improvement of those whom he is teaching. I think our masterships here offer a noble field of duty, and I would not bestow them on any one whom I thought would undertake them without entering into the spirit of our system heart and hand."

it became so thoroughly dependent upon him, and so thoroughly penetrated with his spirit. From one end of it to the other, whatever defects it had were his defects : whatever excellences it had were his excellences. It was not the master who was beloved or disliked for the sake of the school, but the school which was beloved or disliked for the sake of the master. Whatever peculiarity of character was impressed on the scholars whom it sent forth, was derived, not from the genius of the place, but from the genius of the man. Throughout, whether in the school itself, or in its after-effects, the one image that we have before us is not Rugby, but ARNOLD.

What was his great object has already appeared from his letters ; namely, the hope of making the school a place of really Christian education, — words which in his mouth meant something very different from the general professions which every good teacher must be supposed to make, and which no teacher, even in the worst times of English education, could have openly ventured to disclaim, but which it is exceedingly difficult so to explain, as that they shall not seem to exceed or fall short of the truth.

It was not an attempt merely to give more theological instruction, or to introduce sacred words into school admonitions : there may have been some occasions for religious advice that might have been turned to more advantage, some religious practices which might have been more constantly or effectually encouraged. His design arose out of the very nature of his office : the relation of an instructor to his pupils was to him, like all the other relations of human life, only in a healthy state when subordinate to their common relation to God. "The business of a schoolmaster," he used to say, "no less than that of a parish minister, is the cure of souls." The idea of a Christian school, again, was to him the natural result, so to speak, of the very idea of a school in itself, exactly as the idea of a Christian state seemed to him to be involved in the very idea of a state itself. The intellectual training was not for a moment underrated, and the machinery of the school was left to have its own way. But he looked upon the whole as bearing on the advancement of the one end of all instruction and education : the boys were still treated as school-boys, but as school-boys who must grow up to be Christian men ; whose age did not prevent their faults from being sins, or their excellences from being noble and Christian virtues ; whose situation did not of itself make the application of Christian principles to their daily lives an impracticable vision.

His education, in short, it was once observed amidst the vehement outcry by which he used to be assailed, was not (according to the popular phrase) based upon religion, but was itself *religious*. It was this chiefly which gave a oneness to his work amidst a great variety of means and occupations, and a steadiness to the general system amidst its almost unceasing change. It was this which makes it difficult to separate one part of his work from another, and which often made it impossible for his pupils to say, in after-life, of much that had influenced them, whether they had derived it from what was spoken in school, in the pulpit, or in private. And, therefore, when either in direct religious teaching, or on particular occasions, Christian principles were expressly introduced by him, they had not the appearance of a rhetorical flourish, or of a temporary appeal to the feelings; they were looked upon as the natural expression of what was constantly implied : it was felt that he had the power, in which so many teachers have been deficient, of saying what he did mean, and of not saying what he did not mean, — the power of doing what was right, and speaking what was true, and thinking what was good, independently of any professional or conventional notions that so to act, speak, or think was becoming or expedient.

It was not merely an abstract school, but an English public school, which he looked upon as the sphere in which this was to be effected. There was something to him, at the very outset, full of interest in a great place of national education, such as he considered a public school to be.

"There is," he said, "or there ought to be, something very ennobling in being connected with an establishment at once ancient and magnificent, where all about us, and all the associations belonging to the objects around us, should be great, splendid, and elevating. What an individual ought and often does derive from the feeling that he is born of an old and illustrious race, from being familiar from his childhood with the walls and trees which speak of the past no less than of the present, and make both full of images of greatness, this, in an inferior degree, belongs to every member of an ancient and celebrated place of education. In this respect, every one of us has a responsibility imposed upon him, which I wished that we more considered." (Sermons, vol. iii. p. 210.)

This feeling of itself dictated the preservation of the old school constitution as far as it was possible ; and he was very careful not to break through any customs which connected the institution, however slightly, with the past. But, in this constitution, there were peculiarities of far greater importance in his eyes for good or evil, than any mere imaginative associations, — the peculiarities which distinguish the English public-school system from almost every other system of education in Europe, and which are all founded on the fact that a large number of boys are left for a large portion of their time to form an independent society of their own, in which the influence that they exercise over each other is far greater than can possibly be exercised by the masters, even if multiplied beyond their present number.

How keenly he felt the evils resulting from this system, and the difficulty of communicating to it a really Christian character, will be evident to any one who knows the twelfth sermon in his second volume, in which he unfolded, at the beginning of his career, the causes which had led good men to declare that " public schools are the seats and nurseries of vice ; " or the three sermons on " Christian Schools " in his fifth volume, in which, with the added experience of ten years, he analyzed the six evils by which he " supposed that great schools were likely to be corrupted, and to be changed from the likeness of God's temple to that of a den of thieves." (Vol. v. p. 74.)

Sometimes he would be led to doubt whether it were really compatible with the highest principles of education : sometimes he would seem to have an earnest and almost impatient desire to free himself from it. Still, on the whole, it was always on a reformation, not on an overthrow, of the existing constitution of the school that he endeavored to act. "Another system," he said, "may be better in itself; but I am placed in this system, and am bound to try what I can make of it."

With his usual undoubting confidence in what he believed to be a general law of Providence, he based his whole management of the school on his early-formed and yearly-increasing conviction, that what he had to look for, both intellectually and morally, was not performance, but promise ; that the very freedom and independence of school-life, which in itself he thought so dangerous, might be made the best preparation for Christian manhood : and he did not hesitate to apply to his scholars the principle which seemed to him to have been adopted in the training of the childhood of the human race itself. He shrunk from pressing on the conscience of boys rules of action which he felt they were not yet able to bear, and from enforcing actions which, though right in themselves, would in boys be performed from wrong motives.

Keenly as he felt the risk and fatal consequences

of the failure of this trial, still it was his great, sometimes his only, support, to believe that " the character
is braced amid such scenes to a greater beauty and
firmness than it ever can attain without enduring and
witnessing them. Our work here would be absolutely
unendurable if we did not bear in mind that we should
look forward as well as backward — if we did not remember that the victory of fallen man lies not in innocence, but in tried virtue." (Sermons, vol. iv. p. 7.) " I
hold fast," he said, " to the great truth, that ' blessed
is he that overcometh ; ' " and he writes in 1837,
" Of all the painful things connected with my employment, nothing is equal to the grief of seeing a boy
come to school innocent and promising, and tracing
the corruption of his character from the influence of
the temptations around him, in the very place which
ought to have strengthened and improved it. But in
most cases, those who come with a character of positive good are benefited : it is the neutral and indeci-
sive characters which are apt to be decided for evil
by schools, as they would be, in fact, by any other
temptation."

But this very feeling led him with the greater eagerness to catch at every means by which the trial might
be shortened or alleviated. " Can the change from
childhood to manhood be hastened, without prematurely exhausting the faculties of body or mind?"
(Sermons, vol. iv. p. 19) was one of the chief questions
on which his mind was constantly at work, and which,
in the judgment of some, he was disposed to answer

too readily in the affirmative. It was with the elder
boys, of course, that he chiefly acted on this principle ;
but with all above the very young ones, he trusted to
it more or less.   Firmly as he believed that *a* time of
trial was inevitable, he believed no less firmly that it
might be passed at public schools sooner than under
other circumstances ; and in proportion as he disliked
the assumption of a false manliness in boys, was his
desire to cultivate in them true manliness, as the only
step to something higher, and to dwell on earnest
principle and moral thoughtfulness as the great and
distinguishing mark between good and evil.   Hence
his wish, that as much as possible should be done *by*
the boys, and nothing *for* them ; hence arose his practice, in which his own delicacy of feeling and uprightness of purpose powerfully assisted him, of treating
the boys as gentlemen and reasonable beings, of making them respect themselves by the mere respect he
showed to them, of showing that he appealed and
trusted to their own common sense and conscience.
Lying, for example, to the masters, he made a great
moral offence ; placing implicit confidence in a boy's
assertion, and then, if a falsehood was discovered,
punishing it severely — in the upper part of the school,
when persisted in, with expulsion.   Even with the
lower forms, he never seemed to be on the watch for
boys ; and in the higher forms, any attempt at further
proof of an assertion was immediately checked : " If
you say so, that is quite enough — *of course* I believe
your word ; " and there grew up in consequence a

general feeling that "it was a shame to tell Arnold a lie — he always believes one."

Perhaps the liveliest representation of this general spirit, as distinguished from its exemplification in particular parts of the discipline and instruction, would be formed by recalling his manner as he appeared in the great school, where the boys used to meet when the whole school was assembled collectively, and not in its different forms or classes. Then, whether on his usual entrance every morning to prayers before the first lesson, or on the more special emergencies which might require his presence, he seemed to stand before them, not merely as the head master, but as the representative of the school. There he spoke to them as members together with himself of the same great institution, whose character and reputation they had to sustain as well as he. He would dwell on the satisfaction he had in being head of a society where noble and honorable feelings were encouraged, or on the disgrace which he felt in hearing of acts of disorder or violence, such as in the humbler ranks of life would render them amenable to the laws of their country; or, again, on the trust which he placed in their honor as gentlemen, and the baseness of any instance in which it was abused. "Is this a Christian school?" he indignantly asked at the end of one of those addresses, in which he had spoken of an extensive display of bad feeling amongst the boys, and then added, "I cannot remain here if all is to be carried on by constraint and force: if I am to be here as a jailer,

I will resign my office at once." And few scenes can be recorded more characteristic of him than on one of these occasions, when, in consequence of a disturbance, he had been obliged to send away several boys, and when, in the midst of the general spirit of discontent which this excited, he stood in his place before the assembled school, and said, "It is *not* necessary that this should be a school of three hundred, or one hundred, or of fifty boys ; but it *is* necessary that it should be a school of Christian gentlemen."

The means of carrying out these principles were, of course, various : they may, however, for the sake of convenience, be viewed under the divisions of the general discipline of the school, the system of instruction, the chapel services, and his own personal intercourse and influence.

I. In considering his general management of the discipline of the school, it will only be possible to touch on its leading features.

1. He at once made a great alteration in the whole system of punishments in the higher part of the school, "keeping it as much as possible in the background, and by kindness and encouragement attracting the good and noble feelings of those with whom he had to deal." As this appears more distinctly elsewhere, it is needless to enlarge upon it here ; but a few words may be necessary to explain the view with which, for the younger part of the school, he made a point of maintaining, to a certain extent, the old discipline of public schools.

"The *beau-ideal* of school discipline with regard to young boys would seem to be this, that whilst corporal punishment was retained on principle, as fitly answering to and marking the naturally inferior state of boyhood, and, therefore, as conveying no peculiar degradation to persons in such a state, we should cherish and encourage to the utmost all attempts made by the several boys, as individuals, to escape from the natural punishment of their age, by rising above its naturally low tone of principle."

Flogging, therefore, for the younger part, he retained ; but it was confined to moral offences, such as lying, drinking, and habitual idleness; while his aversion to inflicting it rendered it still less frequent in practice than it would have been according to the rule he had laid down for it. But in answer to the argument used in a liberal journal, that it was even for these offences and for this age degrading, he replied with characteristic emphasis, —

"I know well of what feeling this is the expression : it originates in that proud notion of personal independence which is neither reasonable nor Christian, but essentially barbarian. It visited Europe with all the curses of the age of chivalry, and is threatening us now with those of Jacobinism. . . . At an age when it is almost impossible to find a true manly sense of the degradation of guilt or faults, where is the wisdom of encouraging a fantastic sense of the degradation of personal correction? What can be more false, or more adverse to the simplicity, sobriety, and humbleness of mind, which are the best ornament of youth, and the best promise of a noble manhood?"

2. But his object was, of course, far higher than to check particular vices. "What I want to see in the

school," he said, "and what I cannot find, is an abhorrence of evil: I always think of the psalm, 'Neither doth he abhor any thing that is evil.'" Amongst all the causes which, in his judgment, contributed to the absence of this feeling, and to the moral childishness, which he considered the great curse of public schools, the chief seemed to him to lie in the spirit which was there encouraged of combination, of companionship, of excessive deference to the public opinion prevalent in the school. Peculiarly repugnant as this spirit was at once to his own reverence for lawful authority, and to his dislike of servile submission to unlawful authority; fatal as he deemed it to all approach to sympathy between himself and his scholars, to all free and manly feeling in individual boys, to all real and permanent improvement of the institution itself, — it gave him more pain when brought prominently before him, than any other evil in the school. At the very sight of a knot of vicious or careless boys gathered together around the great schoolhouse fire, "It makes me think," he would say, "that I see the Devil in the midst of them." From first to last, it was the great subject to which all his anxiety converged. No half-year ever passed without his preaching upon it; he turned it over and over in every possible point of view; he dwelt on it as the one master-fault of all. "If the spirit of Elijah were to stand in the midst of us, and we were to ask him, 'What shall we do then?' his answer would be, 'Fear not, nor heed one another's voices, but fear and heed the voice of God only.'" (MS. sermon on Luke iii. 10. 1833.)

Against this evil he felt that no efforts of good individual example, or of personal sympathy with individual masters, could act effectually, unless there were something to counteract it constantly amongst the boys themselves.

" He, therefore, who wishes " (to use his own words) "really to improve public education, would do well to direct his attention to this point, and to consider how there can be infused into a society of boys such elements as, without being too dissimilar to coalesce thoroughly with the rest, shall yet be so superior as to raise the character of the whole. It would be absurd to say that any school has as yet fully solved this problem. I am convinced, however, that in the peculiar relation of the highest form to the rest of the boys, such as it exists in our great public schools, there is to be found the best means of answering it. This relation requires, in many respects, to be improved in its character; some of its features should be softened, others elevated; but here, and here only, is the engine which can effect the end desired." (Journ. Ed. p. 292.)

In other words, he determined to use, and to improve to the utmost, the existing machinery of the Sixth Form, and of fagging; understanding by the Sixth Form, the thirty boys who composed the highest class, — "those who, having risen to the highest form in the school, will probably be at once the oldest and the strongest and the cleverest, and, if the school be well ordered, the most respectable in application and general character;" and by fagging, " the power given by the supreme authorities of the school to the Sixth Form, to be exercised by them over the lower boys, for the sake of securing a regular government amongst the boys themselves, and avoiding the evils of anarchy, in other words, of the lawless tyranny of physical strength." (Journ. Ed. pp. 286, 287.)

In many points, he took the institution as he found it, and as he remembered it at Winchester. The responsibility of checking bad practices without the intervention of the masters, the occasional settlement of difficult cases of school government, the subjection of brute force to some kind of order, involved in the maintenance of such an authority, had been more or less produced under the old system, both at Rugby and elsewhere. But his zeal in its defence, and his confident reliance upon it as the keystone of his whole government, were eminently characteristic of himself. It was a point, moreover, on which the spirit of the age set strongly and increasingly against him, on which there was a general tendency to yield to the popular outcry, and on which the clamor, that at one time assailed him, was ready to fasten as a subject where all parties could concur in their condemnation. But he was immovable; and though, on his first coming, he had felt himself called upon rather to restrain the authority of the Sixth Form from abuses, than to guard it from encroachments, yet, now that the whole system was denounced as cruel and absurd, he delighted to stand forth as its champion. The power, which was most strongly condemned, of personal chastisement vested in the Præpostors over those who resisted their authority, he firmly maintained as essential to the general support of the good order of the place; and there was no obloquy which he would not undergo in the protection of a boy who had by due exercise of this discipline made himself obnoxious to the school, the parents, or the public.

But the importance which he attached to it arose from his regarding it not only as an efficient engine of discipline, but as the chief means of creating a respect for moral and intellectual excellence, and of diffusing his own influence through the mass of the school. Whilst he made the Præpostors rely upon his support in all just use of their authority, as well as on his severe judgment of all abuse of it, he endeavored also to make them feel that they were actually fellow-workers with him for the highest good of the school, upon the highest principles and motives — that they had, with him, a moral responsibility and a deep interest in the real welfare of the place. Occasionally during his whole stay, and regularly at the beginning or end of every half-year during his later years, he used to make short addresses to them on their duties, or on the general state of the school, one of which, as an illustration of his general mode of speaking and acting with them, it has been thought worth while to give, as nearly as his pupils could remember it, in the very words he used. After making a few remarks to them on their work in the lessons, "I will now," he proceeded, "say a few words to you, as I prómised. Speaking to you, as to young men who can enter into what I say, I wish you to feel that you have another duty to perform, holding the situation that you do in the school: of the importance of this, I wish you all to feel sensible, and of the enormous influence you possess, in ways in which we cannot, for good or for evil, on all below you; and I wish you to see fully how many and great are the opportunities offered to you here of doing good — good, too, of lasting benefit to yourselves as well as to others; there is no place where you will find better opportunities for some time to come, and you will then have reason to look back to your life here with the greatest pleasure. You will soon find, when you change your life here for that at the universities, how very few in comparison they are there, however willing you may then be, — at any rate during the first part of your life there. That there is good, working in the school, I most fully believe, and we cannot feel too thankful for it: in many individual instances, in different parts of the school, I have seen the change from evil to good — to mention instances would, of course, be wrong. The state of the school is a subject of congratulation to us all, but only so far as to encourage us to increased exertions; and I am sure we ought all to feel it a subject of most sincere thankfulness to God; but we must not stop here; we must exert ourselves with earnest prayer to God for its continuance. And what I have often said before, I repeat now: what we must look for here is, first, religious and moral principles; secondly, gentlemanly conduct; thirdly, intellectual ability."

Nothing, accordingly, so shook his hopes of doing

good, as weakness or misconduct in the Sixth. "You should feel," he said, "like officers in the army or navy, whose want of moral courage would, indeed, be thought cowardice." "When I have confidence in the Sixth," was the end of one of his farewell addresses, "there is no post in England which I would exchange for this; but, if they do not support me, I must go."

It may well be imagined how important this was as an instrument of education, independently of the weight of his own personal qualities. Exactly at the age when boys begin to acquire some degree of self-respect, and some desire for the respect of others, they were treated with confidence by one whose confidence they could not but regard as worth having, and found themselves in a station where their own dignity could not be maintained except by consistent good conduct. And exactly at a time when manly aspirations begin to expand, they found themselves invested with functions of government, great beyond their age, yet naturally growing out of their position; whilst the ground of solemn responsibility, on which they were constantly taught that their authority rested, had a general, though of course not universal, tendency to counteract any notions of mere personal self-importance.

"I cannot deny that you have an anxious duty, — a duty which some might suppose was too heavy for your years. But it seems to me the nobler as well as the truer way of stating the case, to say that it is the great privilege of this and other such institutions, to anticipate the common time of manhood; that by their whole training they fit the character for manly duties at an age when, under another system, such duties would be impracticable; that there is not imposed upon you too heavy a burden, but that you are capable of bearing, without injury, what to others might be a burden; and therefore to diminish your duties, and lessen your responsibility, would be no kindness, but a degradation,—an affront to you and to the school." (Sermons, vol. v. p. 59.)

3. Whilst he looked to the Sixth Form as the ordinary corrective · for the ordinary evils of a public school, he still felt that these evils from time to time developed themselves in a shape which demanded peculiar methods to meet them, and which may best be explained by one of his letters.

"My own school experience has taught me the monstrous evil of a state of low principle prevailing amongst those who set the tone to the rest. I can neither theoretically nor practically defend our public-school system, where the boys are left so very much alone to form a distinct society of their own, unless you assume that the upper class shall be capable of being in a manner μεσιται between the masters and the mass of the boys; that is, shall be capable of receiving, and transmitting to the rest, through their example and influence, right principles of conduct, instead of those extremely low ones which are natural to a society of boys left wholly to form their own standard of right and wrong. Now, when I get any in this part of the school who are not to be influenced,—who have neither the will nor the power to influence others,—not from being intentionally bad, but from very low wit, and extreme childishness or coarseness of character—the evil is so great, not only negatively but positively (for their low and false views are greedily caught up by those below them), that I know not how to proceed, or how to hinder the school from becoming a place of education for evil rather than for good, except by getting rid of such persons. And then comes the difficulty, that the parents who see their sons only at home — that is just where the points of character which are so injurious here are not called into action — can scarcely be brought to understand why they should remove them; and having, as most people have, only the most vague ideas as to the real nature of a public school, they cannot understand what harm they are receiving, or doing to others, if they do not get into some palpable scrape, which very likely they never would do. More puzzling still is it, when you have many boys of this description, so that the evil influence is really very great, and yet there is not one of the set whom you would set down as a really bad fellow if taken alone; but most of them would really do very well if they were not together, and in a situation where, unluckily, their age and size lead them, unavoidably, to form the laws, and guide the opinion, of their society: whereas, they are wholly unfit to lead others, and are so slow at receiving good influences themselves, that they want to be almost exclusively with older persons, instead of being principally with younger ones."

The evil undoubtedly was great; and the difficulty, which he describes, in the way of its removal, tended to aggravate the evil. When first he entered on his post at Rugby, there was a general feeling in the country, that, so long as a boy kept himself from offences sufficiently enormous to justify expulsion, he had a kind of right to remain in a public school; that the worse and more troublesome to parents were their sons, the more did a public school seem the precise remedy for them; that the great end of a public school, in short, was to flog the vices out of bad boys.

Hence much indignation was excited when boys were sent away for lesser offences: an unfailing supply of vicious sons was secured, and scrupulous parents were naturally reluctant to expose their boys to the influence of such associates.

His own determination had been fixed long before he came to Rugby; and it was only after ascertaining that his power in this respect would be absolute, that he consented to become a candidate for the post. The retention of boys who were clearly incapable of deriving good from the system, or whose influence on others was decidedly and extensively pernicious, seemed to him not a necessary part of the trials of school, but an inexcusable and intolerable aggravation of them. "Till a man learns that the first, second, and third duty of a schoolmaster is to get rid of unpromising subjects, a great public school," he said, "will never be what it might be, and what it ought to be." The remonstrances which he encountered, both on public and private grounds, were vehement and numerous. But on these terms alone had he taken his office; and he solemnly and repeatedly declared, that on no other terms could he hold it, or justify the existence of the public-school system in a Christian country.

The cases which fell under this rule included all shades of character, from the hopelessly bad up to the really good, who yet from their peculiar circumstances might be receiving great injury from the system of a public-school, — grave moral offences frequently repeated; boys banded together in sets, to the great harm of individuals or of the school at large; overgrown boys, whose age and size gave them influence over others, and made them unfit subjects for corporal punishment, whilst the low place which, either from idleness or dulness, they held in the school, encouraged all the childish and low habits to which they were naturally tempted. He would retain boys after offences which, considered in themselves, would seem to many almost deserving of expulsion: he would request the removal of others for offences which to many would seem venial. In short, he was decided by the ultimate result on the whole character of the individual, or on the general state of the school.

It was on every account essential to the carrying out of his principle, that he should mark in every way the broad distinction between this kind of removal, and what in the strict sense of the word used to be called expulsion. The latter was intended by him as a punishment and lasting disgrace, was inflicted publicly and with extreme solemnity, was of very rare occurrence, and only for gross and overt offences. But he took pains to show that removal, such as is here spoken of, whether temporary or final, was not disgraceful or penal, but intended chiefly, if not solely, for a protection of the boy himself or his schoolfellows. Often it would be wholly unknown who were thus dismissed, or why; latterly he generally allowed such cases to remain till the end of the half-year, that their removal might pass altogether unnoticed.

This system was not pursued without difficulty : the inconvenience attendant upon such removals was occasionally very great; sometimes the character of the boy may have been mistaken ; the difficulty of explaining the true nature of the transaction to parents was considerable ; an exaggerated notion was entertained of the extent to which this view was carried.

To administer such a system required higher qualifications in a head master than mere scholarship or mere zeal. What enabled him to do so successfully was the force of his character, his determination to carry out his principles through a host of particular obstacles ; his largeness of view, which endeavored to catch the distinctive features of every case ; the consciousness which he felt, and made others feel, of the uprightness and purity of his intentions. The predictions that boys who failed at school would turn out well with private tutors, were often acknowledged to be verified in cases where the removal had been most complained of; the diminution of corporal punishment in the school was necessarily much facilitated ; a salutary effect was produced on the boys by impressing upon them, that even slight offences, which came under the head master's eye, were swelling the sum of misconduct which might end in removal ; whilst many parents were displeased by the system, others were induced to send " as many boys," he said, " and more, than he sent away ; " lastly, he succeeded in shaking the old notion of the conditions under which boys must be allowed to remain at school, and in impressing on others the standard of moral progress which he endeavored himself to enforce.

The following letter to one of the assistant masters expresses his mode of meeting the attacks to which he was exposed on the two subjects last mentioned.

"I do not choose to discuss the thickness of Præpostors' sticks, or the greater or less blackness of a boy's bruises, for the amusement of all the readers of the newspapers; nor do I care in the slightest degree about the attacks, if the masters themselves treat them with indifference. If they appear to mind them, or to fear their effect on the school, the apprehension in this, as in many other instances, will be likely to verify itself. For my own part, I confess that I will not condescend to justify the school against attacks, when I believe that it is going on, not only not ill, but positively well. Were it really otherwise, I think I should be as sensitive as any one, and very soon give up the concern. But these attacks are merely what I bargained for, so far as they relate to my conduct in the school, because they are directed against points on which my 'ideas' were fixed before I came to Rugby, and are only more fixed now; e.g., that the authority of the Sixth Form is essential to the good of the school, and is to be upheld through all obstacles from within and from without, and that sending away boys is a necessary and regular part of a good system, not as a punishment to one, but as a protection to others. Undoubtedly it would be a better system if there was no evil; but, evil being unavoidable, we are not a jail to keep it in, but a place of education where we must cast it out, to prevent its taint from spreading. Meanwhile let us mind our own work, and try to perfect the execution of our own 'ideas,' and we shall have enough to do, and enough always to hinder us from being satisfied with ourselves; but, when we are attacked, we have some right to answer with Scipio, who, scorning to reply to a charge of corruption, said, 'Hoc die cum Hannibale benè et feliciter pugnavi:' we have done. enough good, and undone enough evil, to allow us to hold our assailants cheap."

II. The spirit in which he entered on the instruction of the school, constituting, as it did, the main business of the place, may perhaps best be understood from a particular exemplification of it in the circumstances under which he introduced a prayer before the first lesson in the Sixth Form, over and above the general prayers read before the whole school. On the morning on which he first used it, he said that he had been much troubled to find that the change from attendance on the death-bed of one of the boys in his house to his school-work had been very great: he thought that there ought not to be such a contrast, and that it was probably owing to the school-work not being sufficiently sanctified to God's glory; that, if it was made really a *religious* work, the transition to it from a death-bed would be slight: he therefore intended for the future to offer a prayer before the first lesson, that the day's work might be undertaken and carried on solely to the glory of God and their improvement, — that he might be the better enabled to do his work.

Under this feeling, all the lessons, in his eyes, and not only those which were more directly religious, were invested with a moral character; and his desire to raise the general standard of knowledge and application in the school was as great as if it had been his sole object.

He introduced, with this view, a variety of new regulations; contributed liberally himself to the foundation of prizes and scholarships, as incentives to study,
and gave up much of his leisure to the extra labor of
new examinations for the various forms, and of a
yearly examination for the whole school. The spirit
of industry which his method excited in his better
scholars, and more or less in the school at large, was
considerable; and it was often complained, that their
minds and constitutions were overworked by premature exertion. Whether this was the case more at
Rugby than in other schools, since the greater exertions generally required in all parts of education, it is
difficult to determine. He himself would never allow
the truth of it, though maintaining that it would be a
very great evil if it were so. The Greek union of the
ἀρετὴ γυμναστικὴ with the ἀρετὴ μουσικὴ, he thought
invaluable in education, and he held that the freedom
of the sports of public schools was particularly favorable to it; and, whenever he saw that boys were
reading too much, he always remonstrated with them,
relaxed their work, and, if they were in the upper part
of the school, would invite them to his house in the
half-year or the holidays to refresh them.

He had a strong belief in the general union of
moral and intellectual excellence. "I have now had
some years' experience," he once said in preaching
at Rugby. "I have known but too many of those
who in their utter folly have said in their heart, there
was no God; but the sad sight — for assuredly none

can be more sad — of a powerful, an earnest, and an inquiring mind seeking truth, yet not finding it — the horrible sight of good deliberately rejected, and evil deliberately chosen — the grievous wreck of earthly wisdom united with spiritual folly — I believe that it has been, that it is, that it may be — Scripture speaks of it, the experience of others has witnessed it; but I thank God that in my own experience I have never witnessed it yet: I have still found that folly and thoughtlessness have gone to evil; that thought and manliness have been united with faith and goodness." And in the case of boys, his experience led him, he said, "more and more to believe in this connection, for which divers reasons may be given. One, and a very important one, is, that ability puts a boy in sympathy with his teachers in the matter of his work, and in their delight in the works of great minds; whereas a dull boy has much more sympathy with the uneducated, and others to whom animal enjoyments are all in all." "I am sure," he used to say, "that, in the case of boys, the temptations of intellect are not comparable to the temptations of dulness;" and he often dwelt on "the fruit which I above all things long for, — moral thoughtfulness, — the inquiring love of truth going along with the devoted love of goodness."

But for mere cleverness, whether in boys or men, he had no regard. "Mere intellectual acuteness," he used to say, in speaking (for example) of lawyers, "divested, as it is, in too many cases, of all that is comprehensive and great and good, is to me more revolting

than the most helpless imbecility, seeming to be almost like the spirit of Mephistopheles." Often when
seen in union with moral depravity, he would be inclined to deny its existence altogether : the generation of his scholars to which he looked back with the
greatest pleasure, was not that which contained most
instances of individual talent, but that which had altogether worked steadily and industriously. The university honors which his pupils obtained were very
considerable, and at one time unrivalled by any
school in England ; and he was unfeignedly delighted
whenever they occurred. But he never laid any stress
upon them, and strongly deprecated any system which
would encourage the notion of their being the chief
end to be answered by school education. He would
often dwell on the curious alternations of cleverness
or dulness in school generations, which seemed to
baffle all human calculation or exertion. "What we
ought to do, is to send up boys who will not be
. plucked." A mere plodding boy was above all others
encouraged by him. At Laleham he had once got
out of patience, and spoken sharply to a pupil of this
kind, when the pupil looked up in his face, and said,
"Why do you speak angrily, sir?— indeed, I am doing the best that I can." Years afterwards he used to
tell the story to his children, and said, " I never felt
so much ashamed in my life : that look and that speech
I have never forgotten." And though it would, of
course, happen that clever boys, from a greater sympathy with his understanding, would be brought into

closer intercourse with him, this did not affect his feeling, not only of respect, but of reverence, to those who, without ability, were distinguished for high principle and industry. " If there be one thing on earth which is truly admirable, it is to see God's wisdom blessing an inferiority of natural powers, where they have been honestly, truly, and zealously cultivated." In speaking of a pupil of this character, he once said, " I would stand to that man *hat in hand;* " and it was his feeling after the departure of such a one that drew from him the most personal, perhaps the only personal, praise, which he ever bestowed on any boy in his Sermons. (See Sermons, vol. iii. pp. 352, 353.)

This being his general view, it remains to unfold his ideas of school-instruction in detail.

1. That classical studies should be the basis of intellectual teaching, he maintained from the first. "The study of language," he said, "seems to me as if it was given for the very purpose of forming the human mind in youth ; and the Greek and Latin languages, in themselves so perfect, and at the same time freed from the insuperable difficulty which must attend any attempt to teach boys philology through the medium of their own spoken language, seem the very instruments by which this is to be effected." But a comparison of his earlier and later letters will show how much this opinion was strengthened in later years, and how, in some respects, he returned to parts of the old system, which on his first arrival at Rugby he had altered or discarded. To the use of Latin verse, which

he had been accustomed to regard as "one of the most contemptible prettinesses of the understanding," "I am becoming," he said, "in my old age more and more a convert." Greek and Latin grammars in English, which he introduced soon after he came, he found were attended with a disadvantage, because the rules which in Latin fixed themselves in the boys' memories, when learned in English were forgotten. The changes in his views resulted, on the whole, from his increasing conviction, that "it was not knowledge, but the means of gaining knowledge, which he had to teach;" as well as by his increasing sense of the value of the ancient authors, as belonging really to a period of modern civilization like our own; the feeling that in them, "with a perfect abstraction from those particular names and associations which are forever biasing our judgment in modern and domestic instances, the great principles of all political questions, whether civil or ecclesiastical, are perfectly discussed and illustrated with entire freedom, with most attractive eloquence, and with profoundest wisdom." (Sermons, vol. iii., Preface, p. xiii.)

From time to time, therefore, as in the "Journal of Education" (vol. vii. p. 240), where his reasons are stated at length, he raised his voice against the popular outcry, by which classical instruction was at that time assailed. And it was, perhaps, not without a share in producing the subsequent re-action in its favor, that the one head master who, from his political connections and opinions, would have been supposed most likely to yield to the clamor, was the one who made the most deliberate and decided protest against it.

2. But what was true of his union of new with old elements in the moral government of the school, applies no less to its intellectual management. He was the first Englishman who drew attention in our public schools to the historical, political, and philosophical value of philology and of the ancient writers, as distinguished from the mere verbal criticism and elegant scholarship of the last century. And besides the general impulse which he gave to miscellaneous reading, both in the regular examinations and by encouraging the tastes of particular boys for geology or other like pursuits, he incorporated the study of modern history, modern languages, and mathematics into the work of the school, which attempt, as it was the first of its kind, so it was at one time the chief topic of blame and praise in his system of instruction. The reading of a considerable portion of modern history was effected without difficulty : but the endeavor to teach mathematics and modern languages, especially the latter, not as an optional appendage, but as a regular part of the school business, was beset with obstacles which rendered his plan less successful than he had anticipated; though his wishes, especially for boys who were unable to reap the full advantage of classical studies, were to a great extent answered.

What has been said, relates rather to his system of instruction than to the instruction itself. His personal share in the teaching of the younger boys was

confined to the general examinations, in which he took
an active part, and to two lessons which he devoted in
every week to the hearing in succession every form in
the school. These visits were too transient for the
boys to become familiar with him, but great interest
was always excited ; and, though the chief impression
was of extreme fear, they were also struck by the way
in which his examinations elicited from them whatever they knew, as well as by the instruction which
they received merely from hearing his questions, or
from seeing the effect produced upon him by their
answers. But the chief source of his intellectual as
of his moral influence over the school was through
the Sixth Form. To the rest of the boys he appeared
almost exclusively as a master ; to them he appeared
almost exclusively as an instructor; it was in the
library tower, where he heard their lessons, that his
pupils became first really acquainted with him, and
that his power of teaching, in which he found at once
his main business and pleasure, had its full scope.

It has been attempted hitherto to represent his
principles of education as distinct from himself : but,
in proportion as we approach his individual teaching,
this becomes impracticable ; the system is lost in
the man ; the recollections of the head master of
Rugby are inseparable from the recollections of the
personal guide and friend of his scholars. They will
at once recall those little traits, which, however minute
in themselves, will to them suggest a lively image of
his whole manner. They will remember the glance

with which he looked round in the few moments of silence before the lesson began, and which seemed to speak his sense of his own position and of theirs also, as the heads of a great school; the attitude in which he stood, turning over the pages of Facciolati's "Lexicon," or Pole's "Synopsis," with his eye fixed upon the boy who was pausing to give an answer; the well-known changes of his voice and manner, so faithfully representing the feeling within. They will recollect the pleased look and the cheerful "Thank you," which followed upon a successful answer or translation; the fall of his countenance with its deepening severity, the stern elevation of the eyebrows, the sudden "Sit down" which followed upon the reverse; the courtesy and almost deference to the boys, as to his equals in society, so long as there was nothing to disturb the friendliness of their relation; the startling earnestness with which he would check in a moment the slightest approach to levity or impertinence; the confidence with which he addressed them in his half-yearly exhortations; the expressions of delight with which, when they had been doing well, he would say that it was a constant pleasure to him to come into the library.

His whole method was founded on the principle of awakening the intellect of every individual boy. Hence it was his practice to teach by questioning. As a general rule, he never gave information, except as a kind of reward for an answer, and often withheld it altogether, or checked himself in the very act of uttering it, from a sense that those whom he was ad-

dressing had not sufficient interest or sympathy to
. entitle them to receive it. His explanations were as
short as possible — enough to dispose of the difficulty,
and no more ; and his questions were of a kind to call
the attention of the boys to the real point of every
subject, to disclose to them the exact boundaries of
what they knew, or did not know, and to cultivate a
habit, not only of collecting facts, but of expressing
themselves with facility, and of understanding the
principles on which their facts rested. "You come
here," he said, "not to read, but to learn how to read :"
and thus the greater part of his instructions were inter-
woven with the process of their own minds ; there was
a continual reference to their thoughts, an acknowledgment that, so far as their information and power
of reasoning could take them, they ought to have an
opinion of their own. He was evidently working not
for, but with, the form, as if they were equally interested
with himself in making out the meaning of the passage
before them. His object was to set them right, not
by correcting them at once, but either by gradually
helping them on to a true answer, or by making the
answers of the more advanced part of the form serve
as a medium, through which his instructions might be
communicated to the less advanced. Such a system
he thought valuable alike to both classes of boys. To
those who by natural quickness or greater experience
of his teaching were more able to follow his instructions, it confirmed the sense of the responsible position
which they held in the school, intellectually as well as

morally. To a boy less ready or less accustomed to it, it gave precisely what he conceived that such a character required. "He wants this," to use his own words, "and he wants it daily, not only to interest and excite him, but to dispel what is very apt to grow around a lonely reader not constantly questioned, — a haze of indistinctness as to a consciousness of his own knowledge or ignorance : he takes a vague impression for a definite one, an imperfect notion for one that is full and complete, and in this way he is continually deceiving himself."

Hence, also, he not only laid great stress on original compositions, but endeavored so to choose the subjects of exercises as to oblige them to read, and lead them to think, for themselves. He dealt at once a death-blow to themes (as he expressed it) on "Virtus est bona res," and gave instead historical or geographical descriptions, imaginary speeches or letters, etymological accounts of words, or criticisms of books, or put religious and moral subjects in such a form as awakened a new and real interest in them ; as, for example, not simply "carpe diem," or "procrastination is the thief of time," but, "carpere diem jubent Epicurei, jubet hoc idem Christus." So again, in selecting passages for translation from English into Greek or Latin, instead of taking them at random from "The Spectator" or other such works, he made a point of giving extracts, remarkable in themselves, from such English and foreign authors as he most admired, so as indelibly to impress on the minds of his pupils some of the most striking names and passages in modern literature. "Ha, very good !" was his well-known exclamation of pleasure when he met with some original thought : "is that entirely your own? or do you remember any thing in your reading that suggested it to you?" Style, knowledge, correctness or incorrectness of statement or expression, he always disregarded in comparison with indication or promise of real thought. "I call that the best theme," he said, "which shows that the boy has read and thought for himself; that the next best, which shows that he has read several books, and digested what he has read ; and that the *worst*, which shows that he has followed but one book, and followed that without reflection."

The interest in their work which this method excited in the boys was considerably enhanced by the respect, which, even without regard to his general character, was inspired by the qualities brought out prominently in the ordinary course of lessons. They were conscious of (what was indeed implied in his method itself) the absence of display, which made it clear that what he said was to instruct them, not to exhibit his own powers : they could not but be struck by his never concealing difficulties, and always confessing ignorance ; acknowledging mistakes in his edition of Thucydides ; and on Latin verses, mathematics, or foreign languages, appealing for help or information to boys whom he thought better qualified than himself to give it. Even as an example, it was not without its

use, to witness daily the power of combination and concentration on his favorite subjects which had marked
him, even from a boy, and which especially appeared
in his illustrations of ancient by modern, and modern
by ancient, history.   The wide discursiveness with
which he brought the several parts of their work to
bear on each other; the readiness with which he referred them to the sources and authorities of information, when himself ignorant of it; the eagerness with
which he tracked them out when unknown, — taught
them how wide the field of knowledge really was.   In
poetry it was almost impossible not to catch something
of the delight and almost fervor with which, as he came
to any striking passage, he would hang over it, reading
it over and over again, and dwelling upon it for the
mere pleasure which every word seemed to give him.
In history or philosophy, events, sayings, and authors
would, from the mere fact that he had quoted them,
become fixed in the memory of his pupils, and give
birth to thoughts and inquiries long afterwards, which,
had they been derived through another medium, would
have been forgotten, or remained unfruitful.   The very
scantiness with which he occasionally dealt out his
knowledge, when not satisfied that the boys could
enter into it, whilst it often provoked a half-angry
feeling of disappointment in those who eagerly treas-
ured up all that he uttered, left an impression that
the source from which they drew was unexhausted and
unfathomed, and to all that he did say gave a double
value.

Intellectually as well as morally, he felt that the teacher ought himself to be perpetually learning, and so constantly above the level of his scholars. "I am sure," he said, speaking of his pupils at Laleham, "that I do not judge of them or expect of them as I should if I were not taking pains to improve my own mind." For this reason, he maintained that no schoolmaster ought to remain at his post much more than fourteen or fifteen years, lest by that time he should have fallen behind the scholarship of the age; and by his own reading and literary works he endeavored constantly to act upon this principle himself. "For nineteen out of twenty boys," he said once to Archbishop Whately, in speaking of the importance, not only of information, but real ability, in assistant masters (and his remark, of course, applied still more to the station which he occupied himself), "ordinary men may be quite sufficient; but the twentieth, the boy of real talents, who is more important than the others, is liable even to suffer injury from not being early placed under the training of one whom he can, on close inspection, look up to as his superior in something besides mere knowledge. The dangers," he observed, "were of various kinds. One boy may acquire a contempt for the information itself, which he sees possessed by a man whom he feels, nevertheless, to be far below him. Another will fancy himself as much above nearly all the world as he feels he is above his own tutor, and will become self-sufficient and scornful. A third will believe it to be his duty, as a point of humility, to bring himself down intellectually to a level with one whom he feels bound to reverence; and thus there have been instances where the veneration of a young man of ability for a teacher of small powers has been like a millstone round the neck of an eagle."

His practical talent as a scholar consisted in his insight into the general structure of sentences and the general principles of language, and in his determination to discard all those unmeaning phrases and forms of expression by which so many writers of the last generation, and boys of all generations, endeavor to conceal their ignorance.   In Greek and Latin composition his exceeding indifference to mere excellence of style, when unattended by any thing better, made it difficult for him to bestow that praise which was necessary to its due encouragement as a part of the school work; and he never was able to overcome the deficiency, which he always felt in composing or correcting verse-exercises, even after his increased conviction of their use as a mental discipline.   But to prose composition in both languages he had from the first attached considerable importance, not only as the best means of acquiring a sound knowledge of the ancient authors, but of attaining a mastery over the English language also, by the readiness and accuracy of expression which it imparted.   He retained to himself that happy facility for imitating the style of the Greek historians and philosophers, for which he was remarkable in youth; whilst his Latin prose was peculiar for combining the force of common Latinity with the vigor and simplicity of his own style, — perfectly correct and idiomatic, yet not the language of Cicero or Livy, but of himself.

In the common lessons, his scholarship was chiefly displayed in his power of extempore translation into English. This he had possessed in a remarkable degree from the time that he was a boy at Winchester, where the practice of reading the whole passage from Greek or Latin into good English without construing each particular sentence word by word, had been much encouraged by Dr. Gabell; and in his youthful vacations during his Oxford course, he used to enliven the sick-bed of his sister Susannah by the readiness with which in the evenings he would sit by her side, and translate book after book of the history of Herodotus. So essential did he consider this method to a sound study of the classics, that he published an elaborate defence of it in " The Quarterly Journal of Education; " and when delivering his Modern History lectures at Oxford, where he much lamented the prevalence of the opposite system, he could not resist the temptation of protesting against it, with no other excuse for introducing the subject, than the mention of the Latin style of the middle-age historians. In itself he looked upon it as the only means of really entering into the spirit of the ancient authors; and requiring, as he did, besides, that the translation should be made into idiomatic English, and, if possible, into that style of English which most corresponded to the period or the subject of the Greek or Latin writer in question, he considered it further as an excellent ex-

ercise in the principles of taste and in the knowledge
and use of the English language, no less than of those
of Greece and Rome. No one must suppose that
these translations in the least resembled the para-
phrases in his notes to Thucydides, which are avowedly
not translations, but explanations : he was constantly
on the watch for any inadequacy or redundancy of
expression ; the version was to represent, and no
more than represent, the exact words of the original :
and those who, either as his colleagues or his pupils,
were present at his lessons, well know the accuracy
with which every shade of meaning would be repro-
duced in a different shape, and the rapidity with which
he would pounce on any mistake of grammar or con-
struction, however dexterously concealed in the folds
of a free translation.

In the subject of the lessons, it was not only the
language, but the author and the age, which rose before him : it was not merely a lesson to be got through
and explained, but a work which was to be understood,
to be condemned or to be admired. It was an old
opinion of his, which, though much modified, was never
altogether abandoned, that the mass of boys had not
a sufficient appreciation of poetry to make it worth
while for them to read so much of the ancient poets,
in proportion to prose writers, as was usual when he
came to Rugby. But for some of them he had, besides, a personal distaste. The Greek tragedians,
though reading them constantly, and portions of them
with the liveliest admiration, he thought on the whole

greatly overrated; and still more, the second-rate Latin poets, but whom he seldom used; and some, such as Tibullus and Propertius, never. "I do really think," he said, speaking of these last as late as 1842, "that any examiners incur a serious responsibility who require or encourage the reading of these books for scholarships: of all useless reading, surely the reading of indifferent poets is most useless." And to some of them he had a yet deeper feeling of aversion. It was not till 1835 that he himself read the plays of Aristophanes; and though he was then much struck with the "Clouds," and ultimately introduced the partial use of his Comedies in the school, yet his strong moral disapprobation always interfered with his sense of the genius, both of that poet and Juvenal.

But of the classical lessons generally his enjoyment was complete. When asked once whether he did not find the repetition of the same lessons irksome to him, "No," he said : "there is a constant freshness in them ; I find something new in them every time that I go over them." The best proof of the pleasure which he took in them is the distinct impression which his scholars retained of the feeling, often rather implied than expressed, with which he entered into the several works ; the enthusiasm with which, both in the public and private orations of Demosthenes, he would con-template piece by piece "the luminous clearness" of the sentences ; the affectionate familiarity which he used to show towards Thucydides, knowing, as he did, the substance of every single chapter by itself ; the

revival of youthful interest with which he would recur
to portions of the works of Aristotle ; the keen sense
of a new world opening before him, with which in later
years, with ever-increasing pleasure, he entered into
the works of Plato ; above all, his childlike enjoyment of Herodotus, and that " fountain of beauty and
delight, which no man," he said, " can ever drain
dry," the poetry of Homer. The simple language of
that early age was exactly what he was most able to
reproduce in his own simple and touching translations ;
and his eyes would fill with tears when he came to
the story which told how Cleobis and Bito, as a reward for their filial piety, lay down in the temple, and
fell asleep and died.

To his pupils, perhaps, of ordinary lessons, the most
attractive were the weekly ones on modern history.
He had always a difficulty in finding any work which
he could use with satisfaction as a text-book. " Gibbon, which in many respects would answer the purpose so well, I dare not use." Accordingly, the work,
whatever it might be, was made the groundwork of
his own observations, and of other reading from such
books as the school - library contained. Russell's
"Modern Europe," for example, which he estimated
very low, though perhaps from his own early acquaintance with it at Winchester, with less dislike than
might have been expected, served this purpose for
several years. On a chapter of this he would ingraft,
or cause the boys to ingraft, additional information
from Hallam, Guizot, or any other historian who hap-

pened to treat of the same period; whilst he himself, with that familiar interest which belonged to his favorite study of history and of geography, which he always maintained could only be taught in connection with it, would by his searching and significant questions gather the thoughts of his scholars round the peculiar characteristics of the age or the country on which he wished to fix their attention. Thus, for example, in the Seven Years' War, he would illustrate the general connection of military history with geography, by the simple instance of the order of Hannibal's successive victories; and then, chalking roughly on a board the chief points in the physical conformation of Germany, apply the same principle to the more complicated campaigns of Frederick the Great. Or, again, in a more general examination, he would ask for the chief events which occurred, for instance, in the year 15 of two or three successive centuries, and, by making the boys contrast or compare them together, bring before their minds the differences and resemblances in the state of Europe in each of the periods in question.

Before entering on his instructions in theology, which both for himself and his scholars had most peculiar interest, it is right to notice the religious character which more or less pervaded the rest of the lessons. When his pupils heard him in preaching recommend them " to note in any common work that they read, such judgments of men and things, and such a tone in speaking of them, as are manifestly at

variance with the spirit of Christ" (Sermons, vol. iii.
p. 116), or when they heard him ask "whether the
Christian ever feels more keenly awake to the purity
of the spirit of the gospel, than when he reads the
history of crimes related with no true sense of their
evil" (Sermons, vol. ii. p. 223), instances would immediately occur to them from his own practice, to
prove how truly he felt what he said.   No direct instruction could leave on their minds a livelier image
of his disgust at moral evil than the black cloud of
indignation which passed over his face when speaking
of the crimes of Napoleon or of Cæsar, and the dead
pause which followed, as if the acts had just been committed in his very presence.   No expression of his
reverence for a high standard of Christian excellence
could have been more striking than the almost involuntary expressions of admiration which broke from
him whenever mention was made of St. Louis of
France.   No general teaching of the providential government of the world could have left a deeper impression than the casual allusions to it, which occurred as
they came to any of the critical moments in the history
of Greece and Rome.   No more forcible contrast
could have been drawn between the value of Christianity and of heathenism than the manner with which,
for example, after reading in the earlier part of the
lesson one of the Scripture descriptions of the Gentile
world, "Now," he said, as he opened the "Satires"
of Horace, "we shall see what it was."

Still, it was in the Scripture lessons that this found

most scope.   In the lower forms, it was rather that
more prominence was given to them, and that they
were placed under better regulations, than that they
were increased in amount.   In the Sixth Form, besides
the lectures on Sunday, he introduced two lectures on
the Old or New Testament in the course of the week;
so that a boy who remained there three years would
often have read through a great part of the New Testament, much of the Old Testament, and especially of
the Psalms in the Septuagint version, and also committed much of them to memory: whilst at times he
would deliver lectures on the history of the early
Church, or of the English Reformation.   In these lessons on the Scriptures, he would insist much on the
importance of familiarity with the very words of the
sacred writers, and of the exact place where passages
occurred; on a thorough acquaintance with the different parts of the story contained in the several Gospels,
that they might be referred to at once; on the knowledge of the times when, and the persons to whom, the
Epistles were written.   In translating the New Testament, while he encouraged his pupils to take the language of the authorized version as much as possible,
he was very particular in not allowing them to use
words which fail to convey the meaning of the original,
or which by frequent use have lost all definite meaning
of their own, such as "edification," or "the Gospel."   Whatever dogmatical instruction he gave, was
conveyed almost entirely in a practical or exegetical
shape; and it was very rarely indeed that he made

any allusion to existing parties or controversies within the Church of England.   His own peculiar views, which need not be noticed in this place, transpired more or less throughout ; but the great proportion of his interpretations were such as most of his pupils, of whatever opinions, eagerly collected and preserved for their own use in after-life.

But more important than any details was the union of reverence and reality in his whole manner of treating the Scriptures, which so distinguished these lessons from such as may in themselves almost as little deserve the name of religious instruction as many lessons commonly called secular.   The same searching questions, the same vividness which marked his hostorical lessons, — the same anxiety to bring all that he said home to their own feelings, which made him, in preparing them for confirmation, endeavor to make them say, "Christ died for me," instead of the general phrase, "Christ died for us," — must often, when applied to the natural vagueness of boys' notions on religious subjects, have dispelled it forever.   "He appeared to me," writes a pupil, whose intercourse with him never extended beyond these lessons, "to be remarkable for his habit of realizing every thing that we are told in Scripture.   You know how frequently we can ourselves, and how constantly we hear others, go prosing on in a sort of religious cant or slang, which is as easy to learn as any other technical jargon, without seeing, as it were, by that faculty which all possess of picturing to the mind, and acting as if we really saw things unseen, belonging to another world. Now, he seemed to have the freshest view of our Lord's life and death that I ever knew a man to possess. His rich mind filled up the naked outline of the gospel history: it was to him the most interesting *fact* that has ever happened, — as real, as *exciting* (if I may use the expression), as any recent event in modern history, of which the actual effects are visible." And all his comments, on whatever view of inspiration they were given, were always made in a tone and manner that left an impression, that, from the book which lay before him, he was really seeking to draw his rule of life, and that, whilst he examined it in earnest to find what its meaning was, when he had found it he intended to abide by it.

The effect of these instructions was naturally more permanent (speaking merely in an intellectual point of view) than the lessons themselves ; and it was a frequent topic of censure, that his pupils were led to take up his opinions before their minds were duly prepared for them. What was true of his method and intention in the simplest matters of instruction, was true of it as applied to the highest matters. Undoubtedly, it was his belief that the minds of young men ought to be awakened to the greatness of things around them ; and it was his earnest endeavor to give them what he thought the best means of attaining a firm hold upon truth. But it was always his wish that his pupils should form their opinions for themselves, and not take them on trust from him. To his particular political princi-

ples he carefully avoided allusion; and it was rarely
that his subjects for school compositions touched on
any topics that could have involved, even remotely,
the disputed points of party politics. In theological
matters, partly from the nature of the case, partly from
the peculiar aspect under which for the last six years
of his life he regarded the Oxford school, he both expressed his thoughts more openly, and was more anxious to impress them upon his pupils; but this was
almost entirely in the comparatively few sermons
preached on what could be called controversial topics.
In his intercourse, indeed, with his pupils after they
had left the school, he naturally spoke with greater
freedom on political or theological subjects, yet it was
usually when invited by them; and, though he often
deeply lamented their adoption of what he held to be
erroneous views, he much disliked a merely unmeaning
echo of his own opinions. "It would be a great mistake," he said, "if I were to try to make myself here
into a pope."

It was, however, an almost inevitable consequence
of coming into contact with his teaching, and with the
new world which it opened, that his pupils would often,
on their very entrance into life, have acquired a familiarity and encountered a conflict with some of the
most harassing questions of morals and religion. It
would also often happen, that the increasing reverence
which they felt for him would not only incline them
to receive with implicit trust all that he said in the lessons or in the pulpit, but also to include in their ad-

miration of the man all that they could gather of his general views, either from report or from his published works; whilst they would naturally look with distrust on the opposite notions in religion and politics brought before them, as would often be the case, in close connection with vehement attacks on him, which in most cases they could hardly help regarding as unbounded or unfair. Still, the greater part of his pupils, while at school, were, after the manner of English boys, altogether unaffected by his political opinions; and of those who most revered him, none in after-life could be found who followed his views implicitly, even on the subjects on which they were most disposed to listen to him. But though no particular school of opinion grew up amongst them, the end of his teaching would be answered far more truly (and it may suggest to those who know ancient history, similar results of similar methods in the hands of other eminent teachers) if his scholars learned to form an independent judgment for themselves, and to carry out their opinions to their legitimate consequences, — to appreciate moral agreement amidst much intellectual difference, not only in each other or in him, but in the world at large; — and to adopt many, if not all, of his principles, whilst differing widely in their application of them to existing persons and circumstances.

III. If there is any one place at Rugby more than another which was especially the scene of Dr. Arnold's labors, both as a teacher and as a master, it is the School-chapel. Even its outward forms, from " the very cross at the top of the building," on which he loved to dwell as a visible symbol of the Christian end of their education, to the vaults which he caused to be opened underneath for those who died in the school, must always be associated with his name. "I envy Winchester its antiquity," he said, "and am therefore anxious to do all that can be done to give us something of a venerable outside, if we have not the nobleness of old associations to help us." The five painted windows in the chapel were put up in great part at his expense, altogether at his instigation. The subject of the first of these, the great east window, he delighted to regard as "strikingly appropriate to a place of education," being "the Wise Men's Offering;" and the first time after its erection that the chapter describing the Adoration of the Magi was read in the church service, he took occasion to preach upon it one of his most remarkable sermons, that of "Christian Professions — Offering Christ our Best." (Sermons, vol. iii. p. 112.) And as this is connected with the energy and vigor of his life, so the subject of the last, which he chose himself a short time before his death, is the confession of St. Thomas, on which he dwelt with deep solemnity in his last hours, as in his life he had dwelt upon it as the great consolation of doubting but faithful hearts, and as the great attestation of what was to him the central truth of Christianity, our Lord's divinity. Lastly, the monuments of those who died in the school during his government, and whose graves were the first ever made in the chapel; above all, his own, the monument and grave of the only head master of Rugby who is buried within its walls, — gave a melancholy interest to the words with which he closed a sermon preached on the Founder's day, in 1833, whilst as yet the recently opened vaults had received no dead within them : —

"This roof under which we are now assembled, will hold, it is probable, our children and our children's children; may they be enabled to think, as they shall kneel perhaps over the bones of some of us now here assembled, that they are praying where their fathers prayed; and let them not, if they mock in their day the means of grace here offered to them, encourage themselves with the thought that the place had long ago been profaned with equal guilt; that they are but infected with the spirit of our ungodliness."

But of him especially it need hardly be said, that his chief interest in that place lay in the three hundred boys who, Sunday after Sunday, were collected, morning and afternoon, within its walls. "The veriest stranger," he said, "who ever attends divine service in this chapel, does well to feel something more than common interest in the sight of the congregation here assembled. But if the sight so interests a mere stranger, what should it be to ourselves, both to you and to me?" (Sermons, vol. v. p. 403.) So he spoke within a month of his death; and to him certainly, the interest was increased rather than lessened by its familiarity. There was the fixed expression of countenance, the earnest attention with which, after the service was over, he sat in his place looking at the boys as they filed out one by one, in the orderly and silent arrangement which succeeded, in the latter part of his stay, to the public calling over of their names in the chapel. There was the complete image of his union of dignity and simplicity, of manliness and devotion, as he performed the chapel service, especially when at the communion table he would read, or rather repeat almost by heart, the Gospel or Epistle of the day, with the impressiveness of one who entered into it equally with his whole spirit and also with his whole understanding. There was the visible animation with which, by force of long association, he joined in the musical parts of the service, to which he was by nature wholly indifferent, as in the chanting of the Nicene Creed, which was adopted in accordance with his conviction that creeds in public worship (Sermons, vol. iii. p. 310) ought to be used as triumphant hymns of thanksgiving; or still more in the Te Deum, which he loved so dearly, and when his whole countenance would be lit up at his favorite verse, "When Thou hadst overcome the sharpness of death, Thou didst open the kingdom of heaven to all believers."

From his own interest in the service naturally flowed his anxiety to impart it to his scholars; urging them in his later sermons or in his more private addresses, to join in the responses, at times with such effect, that at least from all the older part of the school the responses were very general. The very course of the ecclesiastical year would often be associated in their minds with their remembrance of the peculiar feeling with which they saw that he regarded the greater festivals, and of the almost invariable connection of his sermons with the services of the day. The touching recollections of those amongst the living or the dead, whom he loved or honored, which passed through his mind as he spoke of All Saints' Day, and, whenever it was possible, of its accompanying feast, now no longer observed, All Souls' Day; and the solemn thoughts of the advance of human life, and of the progress of the human race, and of the Church, which were awakened by the approach of Advent, — might have escaped a careless observer; but it must have been difficult for any one not to have been struck by the triumphant exultation of his whole manner on the recurrence of Easter Day. Lent was marked during his last three years, by the putting up of boxes in the chapel and the boarding-houses, to receive money for the poor, a practice adopted not so much with the view of relieving any actual want, as of affording the boys an opportunity for self-denial and almsgiving.

He was anxious to secure the administration of the rite of confirmation, if possible, once every two years; when the boys were prepared by himself and the other masters in their different boarding-houses, who each brought up his own division of pupils on the day of the ceremony; the interest of which was further enhanced, during his earlier years, by the presence of the late Bishop Ryder, for whom he entertained a great respect, and latterly by the presence of his intimate friend, Archbishop Whately. The Confirmation

Hymn of Dr. Hinds, which was used on these occasions, became so endeared to his recollections, that when travelling abroad, late at night, he would have it repeated or sung to him.   One of the earliest public addresses to the school was that made before the first confirmation, and published in the second volume of his Sermons ; and he always had something of the kind (over and above the bishop's charge), either before or after the regular chapel service.

The Communion was celebrated four times a year. At first some of the Sixth Form boys alone were in the habit of attending : but he took pains to invite to it boys in all parts of the school, who had any serious thoughts ; so that the number, out of two hundred and ninety or three hundred boys, was occasionally a hundred, and never less than seventy.   To individual boys he rarely spoke on the subject, from the fear of its becoming a matter of form or favor ; but in his sermons he dwelt upon it much, and would afterwards speak with deep emotion of the pleasure and hope which a larger attendance than usual would give him. It was impossible to hear these exhortations, or to see him administer it, without being struck by the strong and manifold interest which it awakened in him ; and at Rugby it was, of course, more than usually touching to him from its peculiar relation to the school. When he spoke of it in his sermons, it was evident, that amongst all the feelings which it excited in himself, and which he wished to impart to others, none was so prominent as the sense that it was a com-

munion, not only with God, but with one another, and
that the thoughts thus roused should act as a direct
and especial counterpoise to that false communion and
false companionship, which, as binding one another,
not to good, but to evil, he believed to be the great
source of mischief to the school at large. And when
— especially to the very young boys, who sometimes
partook of the Communion — he bent himself down
with looks of fatherly tenderness, and glistening eyes
and trembling voice, in the administration of the elements, it was felt, perhaps, more distinctly than at
any other time, how great was the sympathy which he
felt with the earliest advances to good in every individual boy.

That part of the chapel service, however, which, at
least to the world at large, is most connected with
him, as being the most frequent and most personal of
his ministrations, was his preaching. Sermons had
occasionally been preached by the head master of
this and other public schools to their scholars before
his coming to Rugby, but (in some cases from the
peculiar constitution or arrangement of the school) it
had never before been considered an essential part of
the head master's office. The first half-year he confined himself to delivering short addresses, of about
five minutes' length, to the boys of his own house.
But from the second half-year he began to preach
frequently; and from the autumn of 1831, when he
took the chaplaincy, which had then become vacant,
he preached almost every Sunday of the school-year

to the end of his life. It may be allowable to dwell
for a few moments on a practice which has since been
followed, whenever it was practicable, in the other
great public schools, and on sermons which, as they
were the first of their kind, will also be probably long
looked upon as models of their kind, in English
preaching. They were preached always in the afternoon, and lasted seldom more than twenty minutes,
sometimes less, — a new one almost every time. "A
man could hardly," he said, "preach on the same
subject, without writing a better sermon than he had
written a few years before." However much they
may have occupied his previous thoughts, they were
written almost invariably between the morning and
afternoon service; and though often under such stress
of time that the ink of the last sentence was hardly
dry when the chapel bell ceased to sound, they contain hardly a single erasure : and the manuscript volumes remain as accessible a treasure to their possessors
as if they were printed.

When he first began to preach, he felt that his chief
duty was to lay bare, in the plainest language that he
could use, the sources of the evils of schools, and to
contrast them with the purity of the moral law of
Christianity. "The spirit of Elijah," he said, "must
ever precede the spirit of Christ." But, as he advanced, there is a marked contrast between the severe
tone of his early sermons in the second volume, when
all was yet new to him, except the knowledge of the evil
which he had to combat, and the gentler tone which

could not but be inspired by his greater familiarity both with his work and his pupils — between the direct attack on particular faults which marks the course of Lent Sermons in 1830, and the wish to sink the mention of particular faults in the general principle of love to Christ and abhorrence of sin, which marks the summary of his whole school experience in the last sermon which he ever preached. When he became the constant preacher, he made a point of varying the more directly practical addresses with sermons on the interpretation of Scripture, on the general principles and evidences of Christianity, or on the dangers of their after-life, applicable chiefly to the elder boys. Amongst these last should be noticed those which contained more or less the expression of his sentiments on the principles to which he conceived his pupils liable hereafter to be exposed at Oxford, and most of which, as being of a more general interest, he selected for publication in his third and fourth volumes. That their proportion to those that are published affords no measure of their proportion to those that are unpublished, may be seen at once by reference to the year's course in the fifth volume, which, out of thirty-four, contains only four which could possibly be included in this class. That it was not his own intention to make them either personal or controversial, appears from an explanation to a friend of a statement which, in 1839, appeared in the newspapers, that he "had been preaching a course of sermons against the Oxford errors." — "The origin of the paragraph was simply this : that I preached two in February, showing that the exercise of our own judgment was not inconsistent with the instruction and authority of the Church, or with individual modesty and humility [viz., the thirty-first and thirty-second in vol. iv.]. They were not in the least controversial, and neither mentioned nor alluded to the Oxford writers. And I have preached only these two which could even be supposed to bear upon their doctrines. ˙ Indeed, I should not think it right, except under very different circumstances from present ones, to occupy the boys' time or thoughts with such controversies." The general principles, accordingly, which form the groundwork of all these sermons, are such as are capable of a far wider application than to any particular school of English opinion, and often admit of direct application to the moral condition of the school. But the quick ears of boys, no doubt, were always ready to give such sermons a more personal character than he had intended, or perhaps had even in his mind at the moment ; and at times, when the fear of these opinions was more forcibly impressed upon him, the allusion, and even mention of the writers in question, is so direct, that no one could mistake it.

But it was, of course, in their direct practical application to the boys, that the chief novelty and excellence of his sermons consisted. Yet, though he spoke with almost conversational plainness on the peculiar condition of public schools, his language never left an impression of familiarity, rarely of personal allusion.

In cases of notorious individual misconduct, he generally shrunk from any pointed mention of them ; and on one occasion, when he wished to address the boys on an instance of untruthfulness which had deeply grieved him, he had the sermon before the regular service, in order to be alone in the chapel with the boys, without the presence even of the other masters. Earnest and even impassioned as his appeals were, himself at times almost overcome with emotion, there was yet nothing in them of excitement. In speaking of the occasional deaths in the school, he would dwell on the general solemnity of the event, rather than on any individual or agitating details ; and the impression thus produced, instead of belonging to the feeling of the moment, has become part of an habitual rule for the whole conduct of life. Often he would speak with severity and bitter disappointment of the evils of the place, yet there was hardly ever a sermon which did not contain some words of encouragement. "I have never," he said in his last sermon, "wished to speak with exaggeration : it seems to me as unwise as it is wrong to do so. I think that it is quite right to observe what is hopeful in us, as well as what is threatening ; that general confessions of unmixed evil are deceiving and hardening, rather than arousing ; that our evil never looks so really dark as when we contrast it with any thing which there may be in us of good." (Sermons, vol. v. p. 460.)

Accordingly, even from the first, and much more in after-years, there was blended with his sterner tone a strain of affectionate entreaty, — an appeal to principles, which could be appreciated only by a few ; exhortations to duties, such as self-denial, and visiting the poor, which some at least might practice, whilst none could deny their obligation. There also appeared most evidently, — what indeed pervaded his whole school life, — the more than admiration with which he regarded those who struggled against the stream of school opinion, and the abiding comfort which they afforded him. In them he saw, not merely good boys and obedient scholars, but the companions of every thing high and excellent, with which his strong historical imagination peopled the past, or which his lively sense of things unseen realized in the invisible world. There were few present in the chapel who were not at least for the moment touched, when, in one of his earliest sermons, he closed one of these earnest appeals with the lines from Milton which always deeply moved him, — the blessing on Abdiel.

But more than either matter or manner of his preaching, was the impression of himself. Even the mere readers of his sermons will derive from them the history of his whole mind, and of his whole management of the school. But to his hearers it was more than this. It was the man himself, there more than in any other place, concentrating all his various faculties and feelings on one sole object, combating face to face the evil with which, directly or indirectly, he was elsewhere perpetually struggling. He was not the preacher or the clergyman, who had left behind all his usual thoughts

and occupations as soon as he had ascended the pulpit.
He was still the scholar, the historian, and theologian,
basing all that he said, not indeed ostensibly, but consciously, and often visibly, on the deepest principles
of the past and present. He was still the instructor
and the schoolmaster, only teaching and educating with
increased solemnity and energy. He was still the
simple-hearted and earnest man, laboring to win others
to share in his own personal feelings of disgust at sin,
and love of goodness, and to trust to the same faith in
which he hoped to live and die himself.

It is difficult to describe, without seeming to exaggerate, the attention with which he was heard by all
above the very young boys. Years have passed away,
and many of his pupils can look back to hardly any
greater interest than that with which, for those twenty
minutes, Sunday after Sunday, they sat beneath that
pulpit, with their eyes fixed upon him, and their attention strained to the utmost to catch every word that
he uttered. It is true, that, even to the best, there was
much, and to the mass of boys, the greater part, of
what he said, that must have passed away from them
as soon as they had heard it, without any corresponding fruits. But they were struck, as boys naturally
would be, by the originality of his thoughts, and what
always impressed them as the beauty of his language ;
and in the substance of what he said, much that might
have seemed useless, because for the most part impracticable to boys, was not without its effect in breaking completely through the corrupt atmosphere of

school opinion, and exhibiting before them once every week an image of high principle and feeling, which they felt was not put on for the occasion, but was constantly living amongst them.   And to all it must have been an advantage, that, for once in their lives, they had listened to sermons which none of them could associate with the thought of weariness, formality, or exaggeration.   On many there was left an impression to which, though unheeded at the time, they recurred in after-life.   Even the most careless boys would sometimes, during the course of the week, refer almost involuntarily to the sermon of the past Sunday, as a condemnation of what they were doing.   Some, whilst they wonder how it was that so little practical effect was produced upon themselves at the time, yet retain the recollection (to give the words of one who so describes himself), that " I used to listen to them from first to last with a kind of awe, and over and over again could not join my friends at the chapel door, but would walk home to be alone ; and I remember the same effects being produced by them, more or less, on others, whom I should have thought hard as stones, and on whom I should think Arnold looked as some of the worst boys in the school."

IV. Although the chapel was the only place in which, to the school at large, he necessarily appeared in a purely pastoral and personal relation, yet this relation extended, in his view, to his whole management of his scholars ; and he conceived it to be his duty and that of the other masters to throw themselves, as much as possible, into the way of understanding and entering into the feelings of the boys, not only in their official intercourse, but always. When he was first appointed at Rugby, his friends had feared that the indifference which he felt towards characters and persons with whom he had no especial sympathy, would have interfered with his usefulness as head master. But in the case of boys, a sense of duty supplied the want of that interest in character, as such, of which, in the case of men, he possessed but little. Much as there was in the peculiar humor of boys which his own impatience of moral thoughtlessness, or of treating serious or important subjects with any thing like ridicule or irony, prevented him from fully appreciating, yet he truly felt, that the natural youthfulness and elasticity of his constitution gave him a great advantage in dealing with them. "When I find that I cannot run up the library stairs," he said, "I shall know that it is time for me to go."

Thus, traits and actions of boys, which to a stranger would have told nothing, were to him highly significant. His quick and far-sighted eye became familiar with the face and manner of every boy in the school. "Do you see," he said to an assistant master who had recently come, "those two boys walking together? I never saw them together before; you should make it an especial point of observing the company they keep: —nothing so tells the changes in a boy's character." The insight which he thus acquired into the general characteristics of boyhood, will not be doubted by any

reader of his sermons; and his scholars used sometimes to be startled by the knowledge of their own
notions, which his speeches to them implied. "Often
and often," says one of them, "have I said to myself,
'If it was one of ourselves who had just spoken, he
could not more completely have known and understood our thoughts and ideas.'" And though it
might happen that his opinion of boys would, like his
opinions of men, be too much influenced by his disposition to judge of the whole from some one prominent feature, and though his fixed adherence to
general rules might sometimes prevent him from making exceptions where the case required it, yet few
could have been long familiar with him without being
struck by the distinctness, the vividness, and, in spite
of great occasional mistakes, the very general truth and
accuracy, of his delineation of their individual characters, or the readiness with which, whilst speaking most
severely of a mass of boys, he would make allowances,
and speak hopefully in any particular instance that
came before him. Often before any other eye had
discerned it, he saw the germs of coming good or
evil, and pronounced confident decisions, doubted at
the time, but subsequently proved to be correct; so
that those who lived with him, described themselves
as trusting to his opinions of boys as to divinations,
and feeling as if by an unfavorable judgment their fate
was sealed.

His relation to the boarders in his own house (called
by distinction the Schoolhouse, and containing between

sixty and seventy boys) naturally afforded more scope for communication than with the rest of the school. Besides the opportunities which he took of showing kindness and attention to them in his own family, in cases of distress or sickness, he also made use of the preparation for confirmation for private conversation with them, and during the later years of his life was accustomed to devote an hour or more in the evening to seeing each of them alone by turns, and talking on such topics as presented themselves, leading them if possible to more serious subjects. The general management of the house, both from his strong dislike to intruding on the privacy even of the youngest, and from the usual principles of trust on which he proceeded, he left as much as possible to the Præpostors. Still, his presence and manner when he appeared officially, either on special calls, or on the stated occasions of calling over their names twice a day, was not without its effect. One of the scenes that most lives in the memory of his schoolhouse pupils is their night-muster in the rudely lighted hall — his tall figure at the head of the files of boys arranged on each side of the long tables, whilst the prayers were read by one of the Præpostors, and a portion of Scripture by himself. This last was a practice which he introduced soon after his arrival, when, on one of those occasions, he spoke strongly to the boys on the necessity of each reading some part of the Bible every day, and then added, that, as he feared that many would not make the rule for themselves, he should for the future always

read a passage every evening at this time. He usually brought in his Greek Testament, and read about
half a chapter in English, most frequently from the
close of St. John's Gospel ; when from the Old Testament, especially his favorite Psalms, the nineteenth,
for example, and the one hundred and seventh, and
the others relating to the beauty of the natural world.
He never made any comment, but his manner of
reading impressed the boys considerably ; and it was
observed by some of them, shortly after the practice
was commenced, that they had never understood the
Psalms before.   On Sunday nights he read a prayer of
his own, and, before he began to preach regularly in
the chapel, delivered the short addresses which have
been before mentioned, and which he resumed, in addition to his other work on Sundays, during the last
year and a half of his life.

With the boys in the Sixth Form his private intercourse was comparatively frequent, whether in the lessons, or in questions of school government, or in the
more familiar relation in which they were brought to
him in their calls before and after the holidays, their
dinners with him during the half-year, and the visits
which one or more used by turns to pay to him in
Westmoreland during part of the vacation.   But with
the greater part of the school, it was almost entirely
confined to such opportunities as arose out of the regular course of school discipline or instruction, and the
occasional invitations to his house of such amongst
the younger boys as he could find any reason or
excuse for asking.

It would thus often happen in so large a number, that a boy would leave Rugby without any personal communication with him at all; and, even in the higher part of the school, those who most respected him would sometimes complain, even with bitterness, that he did not give them greater opportunities of asking his advice, or himself offer more frequently to direct their studies, and guide their inquiries. Latterly, indeed, he communicated with them more frequently, and expressed himself more freely both in public and private on the highest subjects. But he was always restrained from speaking much or often, both from the extreme difficulty which he felt in saying any thing without a real occasion for it, and also from his principle of leaving as much as possible to be filled up by the judgment of the boys themselves, and from his deep conviction, that, in the most important matters of all, the movement must come not from without, but from within. And it certainly was the case, that whenever he did make exceptions to this rule, and spoke rather as their friend than their master, the simplicity of his words, the rareness of their occurrence, and the stern background of his ordinary administration, gave a double force to all that was said.

Such, for example, would be the effect of his speaking of swearing to a boy, not so much in anger or reproof, as assuring him how every year he would learn to see more and more how foolish and disgusting such language was; or, again, the distinction he would point out to them between mere amusement and such as encroached on the next day's duties, when, as he said, " it immediately becomes what St. Paul calls *revelling.*" Such also would be the impression of his severe rebukes for individual faults, showing by their very shortness and abruptness his loathing and abhorrence of evil. " Nowhere," he said, in speaking to some boys on bad behavior during prayers at their boarding-house, — " nowhere is Satan's work more evidently manifest than in turning holy things to ridicule." Such also were the cases in which, more than once, boys, who were tormented while at school with sceptical doubts, took courage at last to unfold them to him, and were almost startled to find the ready sympathy with which, instead of denouncing them as profane, he entered into their difficulties, and applied his whole mind to assuage them. So, again, when dealing with the worst class of boys, in whom he saw indications of improvement, he would grant indulgences which on ordinary occasions he would have denied, with a view of encouraging them by signs of his confidence in them ; and at times, on discovering cases of vice, he would, instead of treating them with contempt or extreme severity, tenderly allow the force of the temptation, and urge it upon them as a proof brought home to their own minds, how surely they must look for help out of themselves.

In his preparation of boys for confirmation, he followed the same principle. The printed questions which he issued for them were intended rather as guides to their thoughts than as necessary to be formally answered; and his own interviews with them were very brief. But the few words which he then spoke — the simple repetition, for example, of the promise made to prayer, with his earnest assurance, that, if that was not true, nothing was true : if any thing in the Bible could be relied upon, it was that — have become the turning-point of a boy's character, and graven on his memory as a law for life.

But, independently of particular occasions of intercourse, there was a deep undercurrent of sympathy which extended to almost all, and which from time to time broke through the reserve of his outward manner. In cases where it might have been thought that tenderness would have been extinguished by indignation, he was sometimes so deeply affected in pronouncing sentence of punishment on offenders, as to be hardly able to speak. "I felt," he said once of some great fault of which he had heard in one of the Sixth Form, and his eyes filled with tears as he spoke, "as if it had been one of my own children ; and, till I had ascertained that it was really true, I mentioned it to no one, not even to any of the masters." And this feeling began before he could have had any personal knowledge of them. "If he should turn out ill," he said of a young boy of promise to one of the assistant masters, and his voice trembled with emotion as he spoke, "I think it would break my heart." Nor were any thoughts so bitter to him as those suggested by the innocent faces of little boys as they first came from home, — nor any expressions of his moral indignation deeper than when he heard of their being tormented or tempted into evil by their companions. " It is a most touching thing to me," he said once in the hearing of one of his former pupils, on the mention of some new-comers, " to receive a new fellow from his father, when I think what an influence there is in this place for evil, as well as for good. I do not know any thing which affects me more." His pupil, who had, on his own first coming, been impressed chiefly by the severity of his manner, expressed some surprise, adding that he should have expected this to wear away with the succession of fresh arrivals. " No," he said : " if ever I could receive a new boy from his father without emotion, I should think it was high time to be off."

What he felt thus on ordinary occasions, was heightened, of course, when any thing brought strongly before him any evil in the school. " If this goes on," he wrote to a former pupil on some such occasion, " it will end either my life at Rugby, or my life altogether." " How can I go on," he said, " with my Roman History? There all is noble and high-minded, and here I find nothing but the reverse." The following extract from a letter to his friend, Sir T. Pasley, describes this feeling.

" Since I began this letter, I have had some of the troubles of school-keeping, and one of those specimens of the evil of boy-nature, which makes me always unwilling to undergo the responsibility of advising any man to send his son to a public school. There has been a system of persecution carried on by

the bad against the good, and then, when complaint was made
to me, there came fresh persecution on that very account; and
divers instances of boys joining in it out of pure cowardice, both
physical and moral, when if left to themselves they would have
rather shunned it. And the exceedingly small number of boys
who can be relied on for active and steady good on these occasions, and the way in which the decent and respectable of ordinary life (Carlyle's 'Shams') are sure on these occasions to
swim with the stream, and take part with the evil, makes me
strongly feel exemplified what the Scripture says about the
strait gate and the wide one, — a view of human nature, which,
when looking on human life in its full dress of decencies and
civilizations, we are apt, I imagine, to find it hard to realize.
But here, in the nakedness of boy-nature, one is quite able to
understand how there could not be found so many as even ten
righteous in a whole city. And how to meet this evil I really
do not know ; but to find it thus rife after I have been [so
many] years fighting against it, is so sickening, that it is very
hard not to throw up the cards in despair, and upset the table.
But then the stars of nobleness, which I see amidst the dark-
ness, in the case of the few good, are so cheering, that one is
inclined to stick to the ship again, and have another good try
at getting her about."

V. As, on the one hand, his interest and sympathy
with the boys far exceeded any direct manifestation of
it towards them, so, on the other hand, the impression
which he produced upon them was derived, not so
much from any immediate intercourse or conversation
with him, as from the general influence of his whole
character, displayed consistently whenever he appeared
before them. This influence, with its consequent
effects, was gradually on the increase during the whole
of his stay. From the earliest period, indeed, the

boys were conscious of something unlike what they had been taught to imagine of a schoolmaster ; and by many, a lasting regard was contracted for him : but it was not till he had been in his post some years, that there arose that close bond of union which characterized his relation to his elder pupils ; and it was, again, not till later still that this feeling extended itself, more or less, through the mass of the school, so that, in the higher forms at least, it became the fashion (so to speak) to think and talk of him with pride and affection.

The liveliness and simplicity of his whole behavior must always have divested his earnestness of any appearance of moroseness and affectation. " He calls us *fellows*," was the astonished expression of the boys when, soon after his first coming, they heard him speak of them by the familiar name in use amongst themselves ; and in his later years, they observed with pleasure the unaffected interest with which, in the long autumn afternoons, he would often stand in the school-field and watch the issue of their favorite games of football. But his ascendency was, generally speaking, not gained, at least in the first instance, by the effect of his outward manner. There was a shortness, at times, something of an awkwardness, in his address, occasioned partly by his natural shyness, partly by his dislike of wasting words on trivial occasions, which to boys must have been often repulsive rather than conciliating ; something also of extreme severity in his voice and countenance, beyond what he was himself at all aware of. With the very little boys, indeed, his manner partook of that playful kindness and tenderness which always marked his intercourse with children : in examining them in the lower forms, he would sometimes take them on his knee, and go through picture-books of the Bible or of English history, covering the text of the narrative with his hand, and making them explain to him the subject of the several prints. But in those above this early age, and yet below the rank in the school which brought them into closer contact with him, the sternness of his character was the first thing that impressed them. In many, no doubt, this feeling was one of mere dread, which, if not subsequently removed or modified, only served to repel those who felt it to a greater distance from him. But in many also, this was, even in the earlier period of their stay, mingled with an involuntary and, perhaps, an unconscious, respect inspired by the sense of the manliness and straightforwardness of his dealings, and still more, by the sense of the general force of his moral character ; by the belief (to use the words of different pupils) in " his extraordinary knack, for I can call it nothing else, of showing that his object in punishing or reproving, was not his own good or pleasure, but that of the boy," — " in a truthfulness — an εἰλικρίνεια — a sort of moral transparency ; " in the fixedness of his purpose, and " the searchingness of his practical insight into boys," by a consciousness, almost amounting to solemnity, that, " when his eye was upon you, he looked into your inmost heart ; " that there was something in his very tone and outward aspect, before which any thing low or false or cruel instinctively quailed and cowered.

And the defect of occasional over-hastiness and vehemence of expression, which during the earlier period of his stay at times involved him in some trouble, did not materially interfere with their general notion of his character. However mistaken it might be in the individual case, it was evident to those who took any thought about it, that that ashy paleness and that awful frown were almost always the expression, not of personal resentment, but of deep, ineffable scorn and indignation at the sight of vice and sin; and it was not without its effect to observe, that it was a fault against which he himself was constantly on the watch, and which, in fact, was in later years so nearly subdued, that most of those who had only known him during that time can recall no instance of it during their stay.

But as boys advanced in the school, out of this feeling of fear " grew up a deep admiration, partaking largely of the nature of awe ; and this softened into a sort of loyalty, which remained even in the closer and more affectionate sympathy of later years." "I am sure," writes a pupil who had no personal communications with him whilst at school, and but little afterwards, and who never was in the Sixth Form, " that I do not exaggerate my feelings when I say, that I felt a love and reverence for him as one of quite awful greatness and goodness, for whom I well remember

that I used to think I would gladly lay down my life ; "
adding, with reference to the thoughtless companions
with whom he had associated, " I used to believe that
I, too, had a work to do for him in the school ; and
I did for his sake labor to raise the tone of the set I
lived in, particularly as regarded himself." It was in
boys immediately below the highest form that this new
feeling would usually rise for the first time, and awaken
a strong wish to know more of him. Then, as they
came into personal contact with him, their general
sense of his ability became fixed, in the proud belief
that they were scholars of a man who would be not
less remarkable to the world than he was to themselves ; and their increasing consciousness of his own
sincerity of purpose, and of the interest which he took
in them, often awakened, even in the careless and indifferent, an outward respect for goodness, and an
animation in their work before unknown to them.
And when they left school, they felt that they had
been in an atmosphere unlike that of the world about
them. Some of those who lamented not having made
more use of his teaching whilst with him, felt that " a
better thought than ordinary often reminded them
how he first led to it ; and in matters of literature
almost invariably found, that, when any idea of seeming originality occurred to them, that its germ was first
suggested by some remark of Arnold ; " that " still,
to this day, in reading the Scriptures, or other things,
they could constantly trace back a line of thought
that came originally from him, as from a great parent

mind." And when they heard of his death, they
became conscious — often for the first time — of the
large place which he had occupied in their thoughts,
if not in their affections.

Such was the case with almost all who were in the
Sixth Form with him during the last ten years of his
life ; but with some who, from peculiar circumstances
of greater sympathy with him, came into more permanent communication with him, there was a yet stronger
bond of union.   His interest in his elder pupils, unlike
a mere professional interest, seemed to increase after
they had left the school.   No sermons were so full of
feeling and instruction as those which he preached on
the eve of their departure for the universities.   It was
now that the intercourse, which at school had been
so broken, and, as it were, stolen by snatches, was at
last enjoyed between them to its full extent.   It was
sometimes in the few parting words — the earnest
blessing which he then bestowed upon them — that
they became for the first time conscious of his real
care and love for them.   The same anxiety for their
good which he had felt in their passage through
school, he now showed, without the necessity of official caution and reserve, in their passage through life.
To any pupil who ever showed any desire to continue
his connection with him, his house was always open,
and his advice and sympathy ready.   No half-year,
after the four first years of his stay at Rugby, passed
without a visit from his former scholars : some of
them would come three or four times a year ; some

would stay in his house for weeks. He would offer to prepare them for their university examinations by previous examinations of his own : he never shrunk from adding any of them to his already numerous correspondents, encouraging them to write to him in all perplexities. To any who were in narrow circumstances, — not in one case, but in several, — he would at once offer assistance ; sometimes making them large presents of books on their entrance at the university ; sometimes tendering them large pecuniary aid, and urging to them that his power of doing so was exactly one of those advantages of his position which he was most bound to use. In writing for the world at large, they were in his thoughts, "in whose welfare," he said, "I naturally have the deepest interest, and in whom old impressions may be supposed to have still so much force, that I may claim from them at least a patient hearing." (Sermons, vol. iv., pref. p. lv.) And when annoyed by distractions from within the school, or opposition from without, he turned, he used to say, to their visits as "to one of the freshest springs of his life."

They, on their side, now learned to admire those parts of his character which, whilst at school, they had either not known or only imperfectly understood. Pupils with characters most different from each other's, and from his own, — often with opinions diverging more and more widely from his as they advanced in life, — looked upon him with a love and reverence which made his gratification one of the brightest re-

wards of their academical studies; his good or evil
fame a constant source of interest and anxiety to
them; his approbation and censure amongst their
most practical motives of action; his example one of
their most habitual rules of life.   To him they turned
for advice in every emergency of life, not so much for
the sake of the advice itself, as because they felt that
no important step ought to be taken without consulting him.   An additional zest was imparted to whatever
work they were engaged in, by a consciousness of the
interest which he felt in the progress of their undertaking, and the importance which he attached to its
result.   They now felt the privilege of being able to
ask him questions on the many points which his school-
teaching had suggested without fully developing; but
yet more, perhaps, they prized the sense of his sympathy and familiar kindness, which made them feel
that they were not only his pupils, but his companions.
That youthfulness of temperament which has been
before noticed in his relation to boys, was still more
important in his relation to young men. . All the new
influences which so strongly divide the students of the
nineteenth century from those of the last, had hardly
less interest for himself than for them; and, after the
dulness or vexation of business or of controversy, a
visit of a few days to Rugby would remind them (to
apply a favorite image of his own) "how refreshing
it is in the depth of winter, when the ground is covered with snow, and all is dead and lifeless, to walk
by the seashore and enjoy the eternal freshness and

liveliness of ocean." His very presence seemed to create a new spring of health and vigor within them, and to give to life an interest and an elevation which remained with them long after they had left him again, and dwelt so habitually in their thoughts, as a living image, that, when death had taken him away, the bond appeared to be still unbroken, and the sense of separation almost lost in the still deeper sense of a life and an union indestructible.

What were the permanent effects of this system and influence, is a question which cannot yet admit of an adequate answer, least of all from his pupils. The mass of boys are, doubtless, like the mass of men, incapable of receiving a deep and lasting impression from any individual character, however remarkable; and it must also be borne in mind, that hardly any of his scholars were called by rank or station to take a leading place in English society, where the effect of his teaching and character, whatever it might be in itself, would have been far more conspicuous to the world at large.

He himself, though never concealing from himself the importance of his work, would constantly dwell on the scantiness of its results. "I came to Rugby," he said, "full of plans for school reform; but I soon found that the reform of a public school was a much more difficult thing than I had imagined." And, again, "I dread to hear this called a religious school. I know how much there is to be done before it can really be called so." "With regard to one's work," he said, "be it school or parish, I suppose the desirable feeling to entertain is, always to expect to succeed, and never think that you have succeeded." He hardly ever seems to have indulged in any sense of superiority to the other public schools. Eton, for example, he would often defend against the attacks to which it was exposed, and the invidious comparisons which some persons would draw between that school and Rugby. What were his feelings towards the improvements taking place there and elsewhere, after his coming to Rugby, have been mentioned already: even between the old system and his own, he rarely drew a strong distinction, conscious though he must have been of the totally new elements which he was introducing. The earliest letters from Rugby express an unfeigned pleasure in what he found existing; and there is no one disparaging mention of his predecessor in all the correspondence, published or unpublished, that has been collected for this work.

If, however, the prediction of Dr. Hawkins at his election has been in any way fulfilled, the result of his work need not depend on the rank, however eminent, to which he raised Rugby School, or the influence, however powerful, which he exercised over his Rugby scholars. And if there be any truth in the following letter from Dr. Moberly, to whose testimony additional weight is given, as well by his very wide difference of political and ecclesiastical opinion, as by his personal experience, first as a scholar at Winchester, and an undergraduate at Oxford, then as the tutor of the most flourishing college in that university, and lastly, in his present position as head master of Winchester, it will be felt, that not so much amongst his own pupils, nor in the scene of his actual labors, as in every public school throughout England, is to be sought the chief and enduring monument of Dr. Arnold's head-mastership at Rugby.

EXTRACT FROM A LETTER OF DR. MOBERLY, HEAD MASTER OF WINCHESTER.

Possibly [he writes, after describing his own recollections as a school-boy] other schools may have been less deep in these delinquencies than Winchester: I believe that in many respects they were. But I did not find, on going to the university, that I was under disadvantages as compared with those who came from other places: on the contrary, the tone of young men at the university, whether they came from Winchester, Eton, Rugby, Harrow, or wherever else, was universally irreligious. A religious undergraduate was very rare, very much laughed at when he appeared; and, I think I may confidently say, hardly to be found among public-school men; or, if this be too strongly said, hardly to be found, except in cases where private and domestic training, or good dispositions, had prevailed over the school habits and tendencies. A most singular and striking change has come upon our public schools, — a change too great for any person to appreciate adequately, who has not known them in both these times. This change is undoubtedly part of a general improvement of our generation in respect of piety and reverence; but I am sure that to Dr. Arnold's personal, earnest simplicity of purpose, strength of character, power of influence and piety, which none who ever came near him could mistake or question, the carrying of this improvement into our schools is mainly attributable. He was the first. It soon began to be matter of observation to us in the university, that his pupils brought quite a different character with them to Oxford than that which we knew elsewhere. I do not speak of opinions: but his pupils were thoughtful, manly-minded, conscious of duty and obligation, when they first came to college; we regretted, indeed, that they were often deeply imbued with principles which we disapproved; but we cordially acknowledged the immense improvement in their characters in respect of morality and personal piety, and looked on Dr. Arnold as exercising an influence for good which (for how many years I know not) had been absolutely unknown to our public schools.

I knew, personally, but little of him. You remember the first occasion on which I ever had the pleasure of seeing him; but I have always felt and acknowledged that I owe more to a few casual remarks of his in respect of the government of a public school, than to any advice or example of any other person. If there be improvement in the important points of which I have been speaking at Winchester (and from the bottom of my heart I testify with great thankfulness that the improvement is real and great), I do declare, in justice, that his example encouraged me to hope that it might be effected, and his hints suggested to me the way of effecting it.

I fear that the reply which I have been able to make to your question will hardly be so satisfactory as you expected, as it proceeds so entirely upon my own observations and inferences. At the same time I have had, perhaps, unusual opportunity for forming an opinion, having been six years at a public school at the time of their being at the lowest, — having then mingled with young men from other schools at the university, having had many pupils from the different schools, and among them several of Dr. Arnold's most distinguished ones; and at last, having had near eight years' experience, as the master of a school which has undergone in great measure the very alteration which I have been speaking of. Moreover, I have often said the very things which I have here written, in the hearing of men of all sorts, and have never found anybody disposed to contradict them.

Believe me, my dear Stanley,

Yours most faithfully,

GEORGE MOBERLY.

LETTERS FROM RUGBY.

TO J. T. COLERIDGE, Esq.

RUGBY, Aug. 29, 1828.

. . . Here we are actually at Rugby, and the school will open to-morrow. I cannot tell you with what deep regret we left Laleham, where we had been so peaceful and so happy, and left my mother, aunt, and sisters for the first time in my life, except during my school and college absences. It was quite "feror exul in altum," etc.; but, then, we both looked upon Rugby as on our Italy, and entered it, I think, with hope and with thankfulness. . . . But the things which I have had to settle, and the people whom I have had to see on business, have been almost endless. To me, unused as I was to business, it seemed quite a chaos. But, thank God, being in high health and spirits, and gaining daily more knowledge of the state of affairs, I get on tolerably well. Next week, however, will be the grand experiment; and I look to it naturally with great anxiety. I trust I feel how great and solemn a duty I have to fulfil, and that I shall be enabled to fulfil it by that help which can alone give the "Spirit of power and love, and of a sound mind;" the three great requisites, I imagine, in a schoolmaster.

You need not fear my reforming furiously; there, I think, I can assure you: but, of my success in introducing a religious principle into education, I must be doubtful; it is my most earnest wish, and I pray God that it may be my constant labor and prayer; but to do this would be to succeed beyond all my hopes; it would be a happiness so great, that I think the world would yield me nothing comparable to it. To do it, however imperfectly, would far more than repay twenty years of labor and anxiety.

Saturday, August 30th. I have been receiving, this morning, a constant succession of visitors; and now, before I go out to return — *August 31st.* I was again interrupted, and now I think that I had better at once finish my letter. I have entered twenty-nine new boys, and have got four more to enter; and I have to-day commenced my business by calling over names, and going into chapel, where I was glad to see that the boys behaved very well. I cannot tell you how odd it seems to me, recalling, at once, my school-days more vividly than I could have thought possible.

TO A PUPIL

(Who had written, with much anxiety, to know whether he had offended him, as he had thought his manner changed towards him).

GRASMERE, July 15, 1833.

. . . The other part of your letter at once gratified and pained me. I was not aware of any thing in my manner to you that could imply disapprobation, and certainly it was not intended to do so. Yet it is true that I had observed, with some pain, what seemed to me indications of a want of enthusiasm, in the good sense of the word, of a moral sense and feeling corresponding to what I knew was your intellectual activity. I did not observe any thing amounting to a sneering spirit: but there seemed to me a coldness on religious matters, which made me fear lest it should change to sneering, as your understanding became more vigorous; for this is the natural fault of the undue predominance of the mere intellect, unaccompanied by a corresponding growth and liveliness of the moral affections, particularly that of admiration and love of moral excellence, just as superstition arises, where it is honest, from the undue predominance of the affections, without the strengthening power of the intellect advancing in proportion. This was the whole amount of my feeling with respect to you, and which has nothing to do with your conduct in school matters. I should have taken an opportunity of speaking to you about the state of your mind, had you not led me now to mention it. Possibly my impression may be wrong, and indeed it has been created by very trifling circumstances; but I am always keenly alive on this point, to the slightest indications, because it is the besetting danger of an active mind, — a much more serious one, I think, than the temptation to mere personal vanity.

I must again say, most expressly, that I observed nothing more than an apparent want of lively moral susceptibility. Your answers on religious subjects were always serious and sensible, and seemed to me quite sincere: I only feared that they proceeded, perhaps too exclusively, from an intellectual perception of truth, without a sufficient love and admiration for goodness. I hold the lines, "nil admirari," etc., to be as utterly false as any moral sentiment ever uttered. Intense admiration is necessary to our highest perfection; and we have an object in the gospel, for which it may be felt to the utmost, without any fear lest the most critical intellect should tax us justly with unworthy idolatry. But I am as little inclined as any one to make an idol out of any human virtue, or human wisdom.

TO JACOB ABBOTT

(Author of "The Young Christian," etc.).

RUGBY, Nov. 1, 1833.

Although I have not the honor of being personally known to you, yet my great admiration of your little book, "The Young Christian," and the circumstance of my being engaged, like yourself, in the work of education, induce me to hope that you will forgive the liberty I am taking in now addressing you. A third consideration weighs with me, and in this I feel sure that you will sympathize, — that it is desirable on every occasion to enlarge the friendly communication of our country with yours. The publication of a work like yours in America was far more delightful to me than its publication in England could have been. Nothing can be more important to the future welfare of mankind, than that God's people, serving him in power and in love, and in a sound mind, should deeply influence the national character of the United States, which in many parts of the Union is undoubtedly exposed to influences of a very different description, owing to circumstances apparently beyond the control of human power and wisdom.

I request your acceptance of a volume of Sermons, most of which, as you will see, were addressed to boys or very young men, and which therefore coincide in intention with your own admirable book. And at the same time I venture to send you a little work of mine on a different subject, for no other reason, I believe, than the pleasure of submitting my views upon a great question to the judgment of a mind furnished morally and intellectually as yours must be.

I have been for five years head of this school. [After describing the manner of its foundation and growth.] You may imagine, then, that I am engaged in a great and anxious labor, and must have considerable experience of the difficulty of turning the young mind to know and love God in Christ.

.   .   .   .

TO CHEVALIER BUNSEN.

I have been much delighted with two American works which have had a large circulation in England, — "The Young Christian," and "The Corner Stone," by a New-Englander, Jacob Abbott. They are very original and powerful; and the American illustrations, whether borrowed from the scenery or the manners of the people, are very striking. And I hear both from India and the Mediterranean, the most delightful accounts of the zeal and resources of the American missionaries, that none are doing so much in the cause of Christ as they are. They will take our place in the world, I think not unworthily, though with far less advantages in many respects, than those which we have so fatally wasted. It is a contrast most deeply humiliating to compare what we might have been with what we are, with almost Israel's privileges, and with all Israel's abuse of them. I could write on without limit, if my time were as unlimited as my inclinations: it is vain to say what I would give to talk with you on a great many points, though your letters have done more than I should have thought possible towards enabling me in a manner to talk with you. I feel no doubt of our agreement: indeed, it would make me very unhappy to doubt it, for I am sure our principles are the same, and they ought to lead to the same conclusions. And so I think they do. God bless you, my dear friend: I do trust to see you again ere very long.

TO A PERSON WHO HAD ONCE BEEN HIS LANDLORD

(And was ill of a painful disorder, but refused to see the clergyman of the parish, or allow his friends to address him on religious subjects).

I was very sorry to see you in such a state of suffering, and to hear from your friends that you were so generally. I do not know that I have any title to write to you: but you once let me speak to you, when I was your tenant, about a subject, on which I took it very kind that you heard me patiently; and, trusting to that, I am venturing to write to you again.

I have myself been blessed with very constant health : yet I have been led to think from time to time, what would be my greatest support and comfort if it should please God to visit me either with a very painful or a very dangerous illness; and I have always thought, that in both, nothing would do me so much good as to read, over and over again, the account of the sufferings and death of Christ, as given in the different Gospels. For, if it be a painful complaint, we shall find that in mere pain he suffered most severely and in a great variety of ways; and, if it be a dangerous complaint, then we shall see that Christ suffered very greatly from the fear of death, and was very sorely troubled in his mind up to the very time almost of his actual dying. And one great reason why he bore all this, was that we might be supported and comforted when we have to bear the same.

But when I have thought how this would comfort me, it is very true that one cannot help thinking of the great difference between Christ and one's self, — that he was so good, and that we are so full of faults and bad passions of one kind or another. So that if he feared death, we must have greater reason to fear it; and so indeed we have were it not for him. But he bore all his sufferings, that God might receive us after our death, as surely as he received Christ himself. And surely it is a comfort above all comfort, that we are not only suffering no more than Christ suffered, but that we shall be happy after our sufferings are over, as truly as he is happy.

Dear Mr. ——, there is nothing in the world which hinders you or me from having this comfort, but the badness and hardness of our hearts, which will not let us open ourselves heartily to God's love towards us. He desires to love us and to keep us; but we shut up ourselves from him, and keep ourselves in fear and misery, because we will not receive his goodness. Oh, how heartily we should pray for one another, and for ourselves, that God would teach us to love him, and be thankful to him, as he loves us! We cannot, indeed, love God, if we keep any evil or angry passion within us. If we do not forgive all who may have wronged or affronted us, God has declared most solemnly that he will not forgive us. There is no concealing this, or getting away from it. If we cannot forgive, we cannot be forgiven. But when I think of God's willingness to forgive me every day, — though every day I offend him many times over, — it makes me more disposed than any thing else in the world, to forgive those who have offended me; and this, I think, is natural, unless our hearts are more hard, than with all our faults they commonly are. If you think me taking a liberty in writing this, I can only beg you to remember, that as

I hope Christ will save me, so he bids me try to bring my neighbors to him also; and especially those whom I have known, and from whom I have received kindness. May Christ save us both, and turn our hearts to love him and our neighbors, even as he has loved us, and has died for us!

TO AN OLD PUPIL.

RUGBY, April 5, 1837.

I take this opportunity to answer your kind and interesting letter, for which I beg you to accept my best thanks. I can hardly answer it as I could wish, but I do not like to delay writing to you any longer. Your account of yourself and of that unhealthy state of body and mind under which you have been laboring, was very touching to me. I rejoice that you were recovering from it, but still you must not be surprised if God should be pleased to continue your trials for some time longer. It is to me a matter of the deepest thankfulness, that the fears, which I at one time had expressed to you about yourself, have been so entirely groundless: we have the comfort of thinking, that with the heart once turned to God, and going on in his faith and fear, nothing can go very wrong with us, although we may have much to suffer, and many trials to undergo. I rejoice, too, that your mind seems to be in a healthier state about the prosecution of your studies. I am quite sure that it is a most solemn duty to cultivate our understandings to the uttermost, for I have seen the evil moral consequences of fanaticism to a greater degree than I ever expected to see them realized; and I am satisfied that a neglected intellect is far oftener the cause of mischief to a man, than a perverted or over-valued one. Men retain their natural quickness and cleverness, while their reason and judgment are allowed to go to ruin; and thus they do work their minds, and gain influence, and are pleased at gaining it; but it is the undisciplined mind which they are exercising, instead of one wisely disciplined. I trust that you will gain a good foundation of wisdom in Oxford, which may minister in after-years to God's glory and the good of souls; and I call by the name of wisdom, — knowledge, rich and varied, digested and combined, and pervaded through and through by the light of the Spirit of God. Remember the words, " Every scribe instructed to the kingdom of God is like unto a householder, who bringeth out of his treasure things *new and old;* " that is, who does not think that either the four first centuries on the one hand, nor the nineteenth century on the other, have a monopoly of truth, but who combines a knowledge of one with that of the other, and judges all according to the judgment which he has gained from the teaching of the Scriptures. I am obliged to write more shortly than I could wish: let me hear from you when you can, and see you when you can; and be sure, that, whether my judgments be right or wrong, you have no friend who more earnestly would wish to assist you in that only narrow road to life eternal, which I feel sure that you by God's grace are now treading.

TO AN OLD PUPIL, ENGAGED IN BUSINESS.

Rugby, Nov. 18, 1840.

I think that even your very kind and handsome gift to the library has given me less pleasure than the letter which accompanied it, and which was one of the highest gratifications that a man in my profession can ever experience. Most sincerely do I thank you for it, and be assured that I do value it very deeply. Your letter holds out to me another prospect which interests me very deeply. I have long felt a very deep concern about the state of our manufacturing population, and have seen how enormous was the work to be done there, and how much good men, especially those who were not clergymen, were wanted to do it. And, therefore, I think of you as engaged in business, with no little satisfaction, being convinced that a good man, highly educated, cannot possibly be in a more important position in this kingdom than as one of the heads of a great manufacturing establishment. I feel encouraged also, by the kindness of your letter, to trouble you, perhaps, hereafter with some questions on a point where my practical knowledge is, of course, nothing. Yet I see the evils and dangers of the present state of things, and long that those who have the practical knowledge could be brought steadily and systematically to consider the possibility of a remedy. . . . We are now in the midst of the winter examination, which, as you may remember, gives us all sufficient employment.

TO ARCHBISHOP WHATELY.

I must conclude with a more delightful subject, — my most dear and blessed sister. I never saw a more perfect instance of the spirit of power and of love, and of a sound mind; intense love, almost to the annihilation of selfishness — a daily martyrdom for twenty years, during which she adhered to her early-formed resolution of never talking about herself; thoughtful about the very pins and ribbons of my wife's dress, about the making of a doll's cap for a child — but of herself, save only as regarded her ripening in all goodness, wholly thoughtless, enjoying every thing lovely, graceful, beautiful, highminded, whether in God's works or man's, with the keenest relish; inheriting the earth to the very fulness of the promise, though never leaving her crib, nor changing her posture; and preserved through the very valley of the shadow of death, from all fear or impatience, or from every cloud of impaired reason, which might mar the beauty of Christ's Spirit's glorious work. May God grant that I might come but within one hundred degrees of her place in glory. God bless you all.

TO MR. JUSTICE COLERIDGE.

Fox How, Jan. 2, 1841.

. . . If our minds were comprehensive enough, and life were long enough, to follow with pleasure every pursuit not sinful, I can fancy that it would be better to like shooting than not to like it; but as things are, all our life must be a selection, and pursuits must be neglected, because we have not time or mind to spare for them. So that I cannot but think, that shooting and fishing, in our state of society, must always be indulged at the expense of something better.

I feel quite as strongly as you do the extreme difficulty of giving to girls what really deserves the name of education intellectually. When —— was young, I used to teach her some Latin with her brothers, and that has been, I think, of real use to her; and she feels it now in reading and translating German, of which she does a great deal. But there is nothing for girls like the Degree examination, which concentrates one's reading so beautifully, and makes one master a certain number of books perfectly. And unless we had a domestic examination for young ladies to be passed before they came out, and another like the great go, before they come of age, I do not see how the thing can ever be effected. Seriously, I do not see how we can supply sufficient encouragement for systematic and laborious reading, or how we can insure many things being retained at once fully in the mind, when we are wholly without the machinery which we have for our boys. I do nothing now with my girls regularly, owing to want of time: once, for a little while, I used to examine —— in Guizot's "Civilization of France;" and I am inclined to think that few better books could be found for the purpose than this and his "Civilization of Europe." They embrace a great multitude of subjects, and a great variety, and some philosophical questions among the rest, which would introduce a girl's mind a little to that world of thought to which we were introduced by our Aristotle.

CHAPTER IV.

GENERAL LIFE AT RUGBY.

THE general view of Dr. Arnold's life at Rugby must not be closed without touching, however briefly and imperfectly, on that aspect of it which naturally gave the truest view of his mind and character, whilst to those at a distance it was comparatively but little known.

Perhaps the scene which, to those who knew him best, would bring together the recollections of his public and private life in the most lively way, was his study at Rugby. There he sat at his work, with no attempt at seclusion, — conversation going on around him ; his children playing in the room ; his frequent guests, whether friends or former pupils, coming in or out at will, — ready at once to break off his occupations to answer a question, or to attend to the many interruptions to which he was liable ; and from these interruptions, or from his regular avocations, at the few odd hours or minutes which he could command, would he there return and recommence his writing, as if it had not been broken off. " Instead of feeling my head exhausted," he would sometimes say after the day's business was over, "it seems to have quite an eagerness to set to work." " I feel as if I could dictate to twenty secretaries at once."

Yet, almost unfailing as was this "unhasting, unresting diligence," to use the expression of a keen observer, who thus characterized his impression of one day's visit at Rugby, he would often wish for something more like leisure and repose. "We sometimes feel," he said, "as if we should like to run our heads into a hole — to be quiet for a little time from the stir of so many human beings which greets us from morning to evening." And it was from amidst this chaos of employments that he turned, with all the delight of which his nature was capable, to what he often dwelt upon as the rare, the unbroken, the almost awful happiness of his domestic life. It is impossible adequately to describe the union of the whole family round him, who was not only the father and guide, but the elder brother and playfellow, of his children ; the first feelings of enthusiastic love and watchful care, carried through twenty-two years of wedded life, — the gentleness and devotion which marked his whole feeling and manner in the privacy of his domestic intercourse. Those who had known him only in the school, can remember the kind of surprise with which they first witnessed his tenderness and playfulness. Those who had known him only in the bosom of his family, found it difficult to conceive how his pupils or the world at large should have formed to themselves so stern an image of one in himself so loving. Yet both were alike natural to him; the severity and the playfulness expressing each in their turn the earnestness with which he entered into the business of life, and the enjoyment with which he entered into its rest; whilst the common principle, which linked both together, made every closer approach to him in his private life a means for better understanding him in his public relations.

Enough, however, may perhaps be said to recall something at least of its outward aspect. There were his hours of thorough relaxation, when he would throw off all thoughts of the school and of public matters; his quiet walks by the side of his wife's pony, when he would enter into the full enjoyment of air and exercise, and the outward face of nature, observing with distinct pleasure each symptom of the burst of spring or of the richness of summer — "feeling like a horse pawing the ground, impatient to be off," — "as if the very act of existence was an hourly pleasure to him." There was the cheerful voice that used to go sounding through the house in the early morning, as he went round to call his children; the new spirits which he seemed to gather from the mere glimpses of them in the midst of his occupations; the increased merriment of all in any game in which he joined; the happy walks on which he would take them in the fields and hedges, hunting for flowers; the yearly excursions to look in a neighboring clay-pit for the earliest colt's-foot, with the mock siege that followed. Nor, again, was the sense of his authority as a father ever lost in his

playfulness as a companion. His personal superin-
tendence of their ordinary instructions was necessarily
limited by his other engagements, but it was never
wholly laid aside : in the later years of his life it was
his custom to read the Psalms and Lessons of the
day with his family every morning ; and the common
reading of a chapter in the Bible every Sunday evening, with repetition of hymns or parts of Scripture, by
every member of the family ; the devotion with which
he would himself repeat his favorite poems from " The
Christian Year," or his favorite passages from the
Gospels ; the same attitude of deep attention in
listening to the questions of his youngest children ;
the same reverence in answering their difficulties,
that he would have shown to the most advanced of his
friends or his scholars, — form a picture not soon to
pass away from the mind of any one who was ever
present. But his teaching in his family was naturally
not confined to any particular occasions : they looked
to him for information and advice at all times, and a
word of authority from him was a law not to be questioned for a moment. And with the tenderness which
seemed to be alive to all their wants and wishes, there
was united that peculiar sense of solemnity with which
in his eyes the very idea of a family life was invested.
" I do not wonder," he said, " that it was thought a
great misfortune to die childless in old times, when
they had not fuller light — it seems so completely
wiping a man out of existence." The anniversaries
of domestic events, the passing away of successive

generations, the entrance of his sons on the several stages of their education, — struck on the deepest chords of his nature, and made him blend with every prospect of the future, the keen sense of the continuance (so to speak) of his own existence in the good and evil fortunes of his children, and to unite the thought of them with the yet more solemn feeling with which he was at all times wont to regard " the blessing " of " a whole house transplanted entire from earth to heaven, without one failure."

In his own domestic happiness he never lost sight of his early friends. " He was attached to his family," it was truly said of him by Archbishop Whately, as if he had no friends ; to his friends, as if he had no family ; and," he adds, " to his country, as if he had no friends or relations." Debarred as he was from frequent intercourse with most of them by his and their occupations, he made it part of the regular business of his life to keep up a correspondence with them. " I never do," he said, " and I trust I never shall, excuse myself for not writing to old and dear friends, for it is really a duty which it is mere indolence and thoughtlessness to neglect." The very aspect of their several homes lived as distinct images in his mind, and seemed to have an equal claim on his interest. To men of such variety of opinion and character, that the very names of some of them àre identified with measures and views the most opposite that good men can entertain, he retained to the end a strong and almost equal affection. The absence of greater mutual sympathy was to him almost the only shadow thrown over his happy life; no difference of opinion ever destroyed his desire for intercourse with them; and where, in spite of his own efforts to continue it, it was so interrupted, the subject was so painful to him, that, even with those most intimate with him, he could hardly bear to allude to it.

How lively was his interest in the state of England generally, and especially of the lower orders, will appear elsewhere. But the picture of his ordinary life would be incomplete without mention of his intercourse with the poor. He purposely abstained, as will be seen, from mixing much in the affairs of the town and neighborhood of Rugby. But he was always ready to assist in matters of local charity or usefulness, — giving lectures, for example, before the Mechanics' Institutes at Rugby and Lutterworth, writing tracts on the appearance of the cholera in the vicinity, and, after the establishment of the railway station at half a mile from the town, procuring the sanction of the bishop for the performance of a short service there on Sunday by himself and the assistant masters in turn. And with the poor generally, though his acquaintance was naturally much more limited than it had been in the village of Laleham, yet with some few, chiefly aged persons in the almshouse of the place, he made a point of keeping up a frequent and familiar intercourse.

In this intercourse, sometimes in conversations with them as he met or overtook them alone on the road, usually in such visits as he could pay to them in his spare moments of relaxation, he assumed less of the character of a teacher than most clergymen would have thought right, reading to them occasionally, but generally talking to them with the manner of a friend and an equal. This resulted partly from the natural reserve and shyness which made him shrink from entering on sacred subjects with comparative strangers, and which, though he latterly somewhat overcame it, almost disqualified him, in his own judgment, from taking charge of a parish. But it was also the effect of his reluctance to address them in a more authoritative or professional tone than he would have used towards persons of his own rank. Feeling keenly what seemed to him at once the wrong and the mischief done by the too wide separation between the higher and lower orders, he wished to visit them " as neighbors, without always seeming bent on relieving or instructing them," and could not bear to use language which to any one in a higher station would have been thought an interference. With the servants of his household, for the same reasons, he was in the habit, whether in travelling or in his own house, of consulting their accommodation, and speaking to them familiarly, as to so many members of the domestic circle. And in all this, writes one who knew well his manner to the poor, " there was no affectation of condescension : it was a manly address to his fellow-men, as man addressing man." " I never knew such a humble man as the Doctor," said the parish clerk at Laleham, after he had revisited it from Rugby: "he comes and shakes us by the hand as if he was one of us." "He used to come into my house," said an old woman near his place in Westmoreland, "and talk to me as if I was a lady." Often, no doubt, this was not appreciated by the poor, and might, at times, be embarrassing to himself; and it is said that he was liable to be imposed upon by them, and greatly to overrate their proficiency in moral and religious excellence. But he felt this intercourse to be peculiarly needful for one engaged in occupations such as his: to the remembrance of the good poor, whom he visited at Rugby, he often recurred when absent from them; and nothing can exceed the regret which they testify at his loss, and the grateful affection with which they still speak of him, pointing with delight to the seat which he used to occupy by their firesides; one of them especially, an old almswoman, who died a few months after his own decease, up to the last moment of consciousness never ceasing to think of his visits to her, and of the hope with which she looked forward now to seeing his face once more again.

Closely as he was bound to Rugby by these and similar bonds of social and familiar life, and yet more closely by the charm with which its mere outward aspect and localities were invested by his interest in the school, both as an independent institution and as his own sphere of duty, yet the place in itself never had the same strong hold on his ⌐   ¬
or Laleham; and his ʰ˙ ˙   ...ays spent

away from Rugby, either in short tours, or in later years at his Westmoreland home, Fox How, a small estate between Rydal and Ambleside, which he purchased in 1832, with the view of providing for himself a retreat, in case of his retirement from the school, or for his family in case of his death. The monotonous character of the midland scenery of Warwickshire was to him, with his strong love of natural beauty and variety, absolutely repulsive : there was something almost touching in the eagerness with which, amidst that "endless succession of fields and hedge-rows," he would make the most of any features of a higher order; in the pleasure with which he would cherish the few places where the current of the Avon was perceptible, or where a glimpse of the horizon could be discerned ; in the humorous despair with which he would gaze on the dull expanse of fields eastward from Rugby. "It is no wonder we do not like looking that way, when one considers that there is nothing fine between us and the Ural Mountains. Conceive what you look over ; for you just miss Sweden, and look over Holland, the north of Germany, and the centre of Russia." With this absence of local attraction in the place, and with the conviction that his occupations and official station must make him look for his future home elsewhere, "I feel," he said, "that I love Middlesex and Westmoreland, but I care nothing for Warwickshire, and am in it like a plant sunk in the ground in a pot : my roots never strike beyond the pot, and I could be transplanted at any minute without tearing or severing of my fibres. To the pot itself, which is the school, I could cling very lovingly, were it not that the laborious nature of the employment makes me feel that it can be only temporary, and that, if I live to old age, my age could not be spent in my present situation."

Fox How, accordingly, became more and more the centre of all his local and domestic affections. " It is with a mixed feeling of solemnity and tenderness," he said, " that I regard our mountain nest, whose surpassing sweetness, I think I may safely say, adds a positive happiness to every one of my waking hours passed in it." When absent from it, it still, he said, "dwelt in his memory as a vision of beauty from one vacation to another ; " and when present at it, he felt that "no hasty or excited admiration of a tourist could be compared with the quiet and hourly delight of having the mountains and streams as familiar objects, connected with the enjoyments of home, one's family, one's books, and one's friends," — "associated with our work-day thoughts as well as our gala-day ones."

Then it was that, as he sat working in the midst of his family, " never raising his eyes from the paper to the window without an influx of ever new delights," he found that leisure for writing which he so much craved at Rugby. Then it was that he enjoyed the entire relaxation which he so much needed after his school occupations, whether in the journeys of coming and returning, — those long journeys, which, before they were shortened by railway travelling, were to him, he

used to say, the twelve most restful days of the whole
year, — or in the birthday festivities of his children,
and the cheerful evenings when all subjects were discussed, from the gravest to the lightest, and when he
would read to them his favorite stories from Herodotus, or his favorite English poets. Most of all, perhaps, was to be observed his delight in those long
mountain-walks, when they would start with their pro-
visions for the day, himself the guide and life of the
party, always on the look-out how best to break the
ascent by gentle stages, comforting the little ones in
their falls, and helping forward those who were tired,
himself always keeping with the laggers, that none
might strain their strength by trying to be in front
with him; and then, when his assistance was not
wanted, the liveliest of all; his step so light, his eye so
quick in finding flowers to take home to those who
were not of the party.

Year by year bound him with closer ties to his new
home: not only Fox How itself with each particular
tree, the growth of which he had watched, and each
particular spot in the grounds, associated by him with
the playful names of his nine children, but also the
whole valley in which it lay, became consecrated with
something of a domestic feeling. Rydal Chapel, with
the congregation to which he had so often preached;
the new circle of friends and acquaintance with whom
he kept up so familiar an intercourse; the gorges
and rocky pools which owed their nomenclature to
him, — all became part of his habitual thoughts.

He delighted to derive his imagery from the hills and lakes of Westmoreland, and to trace in them the likenesses of his favorite scenes in poetry and history: even their minutest features were of a kind that were most attractive to him; "the running streams" which were to him "the most beautiful objects in nature;" the wild-flowers on the mountain sides, which were to him, he said, "his music," and which, whether in their scarcity at Rugby, or their profusion in Westmoreland, "loving them," as he used to say, "as a child loves them," he could not bear to see removed from their natural places by the wayside, where others might enjoy them as well as himself. The very peacefulness of all the historical and moral associations of the scenery — free alike from the remains of feudal ages in the past, and suggesting comparatively so little of suffering or evil in the present — rendered doubly grateful to him the refreshment which he there found from the rough world in the school, or the sad feelings awakened in his mind by the thoughts of his Church and country. There he hoped, when the time should have come for his retreat from Rugby, to spend his declining years. Other visions, indeed, of a more practical and laborious life, from time to time passed before him : but Fox How was the image which most constantly presented itself to him in all prospects for the future; there he intended to have lived in peace, maintaining his connection with the rising generation by receiving pupils from the Universities; there, under the shade of the trees of his own planting, he hoped in his old age to give to the world the fruits of his former experience and labors, by executing those works for which at Rugby he felt himself able only to prepare the way, or lay the first foundations, and never again leave his retirement till (to use his own expression) "his bones should go to Grasmere churchyard, to lie under the yews which Wordsworth planted, and to have the Rotha, with its deep and silent pools, passing by."

CHAPTER V.

LAST YEAR, 1842.

IT was now the fourteenth year of Dr. Arnold's stay at Rugby, — a year, on every account, of peculiar interest to himself and his scholars. It had opened with an unusual mortality in the school. One of his colleagues, and seven of his pupils, mostly from causes unconnected with each other, had been carried off within its first quarter ; and the return of the boys had been delayed beyond the accustomed time in consequence of a fever lingering in Rugby, during which period he had a detachment of the higher forms residing near or with him at Fox How. It was during his stay here that he received from Lord Melbourne the offer of the Regius Professorship of Modern History at Oxford, vacant by the death of Dr. Nares. How joyfully he caught at this unexpected realization of his fondest hopes for his latest years, and how bright a·gleam it imparted to the sunset of his life, will best be expressed by his own letters and by the account of his Lectures.

TO THE REV. DR. HAWKINS.

You may perhaps have heard my news already; but I must tell you myself, because you are so much connected with my pleasure in it. I have accepted the Regius Professorship of Modern History, chiefly to gratify my earnest longing to have some direct connection with Oxford; and I have thought with no small delight that I should now see something of you in the natural course of things every year, for my wife and myself hope to take lodgings for ten days or a fortnight every Lent Term, at the end of our Christmas holidays, for me to give my lectures. I could not resist the temptation of accepting the office, though it will involve some additional work; and if I live to leave Rugby, the income, though not great, will be something to us when we are poor people at Fox How. But to get a regular situation in Oxford would have tempted me, I believe, had it been accompanied by no salary at all.

I go up to Oxford on the 2d of December, Thursday week, to read my inaugural lecture. I suppose it is too much to hope that you could be there, but it would give me the greatest pleasure to utter my first words in Oxford in your hearing. I am going to give a general sketch first of the several parts of history generally, and their relation to each other, and then of the peculiarities of modern history. This will do very well for an inaugural lecture; but what to choose for my course after we return from Fox How I can scarcely tell, considering how little time I shall have for any deep research, and how important it is at the same time that my first lectures should not be superficial. . . . Our examination begins on Wednesday; still, as "Thucydides" is done, and gone to the press, and as my lecture will be finished, I hope, in one or two evenings more, I expect to be able to go on again with my history before the end of the week; and I may do a little in it before we go to Fox How.

On the 2d of December he entered on his professorial duties by delivering his inaugural lecture. His school work not permitting him to be absent more than one whole day, he left Rugby with Mrs. Arnold, very early in the morning, and, occupying himself from the time it became light in looking over the school exercises, reached Oxford at noon. The day had been looked forward to with eager expectation : and the usual lecture-rooms in the Clarendon Buildings being unable to contain the crowds that, to the number of four or five hundred, flocked to hear him, the "Theatre" was used for the occasion ; and there, its whole area and lower galleries entirely filled, the professor arose from his place, amidst the highest university authorities in their official seats, and in that clear, manly voice, which so long retained its hold on the memory of those who heard it, began, amidst deep silence, the opening words of his inaugural lecture.

. . . .

The time which he had originally fixed for his retirement from Rugby was now drawing near ; and the new sphere opened to him in his professorship at Oxford, seemed to give a fixedness to his future prospects, which would naturally increase his long-cherished wishes of greater leisure and repose. But he still felt himself in the vigor of life, and used to rejoice in the thought that the forty-ninth year, fixed by Aristotle as the acme of the human faculties, lay still some years before him. The education of his two younger sons was a strong personal inducement to him to remain a short time longer in his situation. His professorial labors were, of course, but an appendage to his duties in the school ; and when some of the unforeseen details of the entrance on his new office had seemed likely to deprive him of the place which he had so delighted to receive, — "in good and sober truth," he writes to Archbishop Whately, " I believe that this and all other things are ordered far more wisely than I could order them, and it will seem a manifest call to turn my mind more closely to the great work which is before me here at Rugby." The unusual amount also of sickness and death which had marked the beginning of the school year, naturally gave an increased earnestness to his dealings with the boys. His latest scholars were struck by the great freedom and openness with which he spoke to them on more serious subjects ; the more directly practical applications which he made of their Scriptural lessons ; the emphasis with which he called their attention to the contrast between Christian faith and love, and that creed of later paganism, which made "the feelings of man towards the Deity to be exactly those with which we gaze at a beautiful sunset." The same cause would occasion those frequent thoughts of death which appear in his chapel sermons, and in his more private life during this last year. There had never, indeed, been a time from his earliest manhood, in which the uncertainty of human life had not been one of the fixed images of his mind ; and many instances would recur to all who knew him, of the way in which it was constantly blended with all his thoughts of the future. "Shall. I tell you, my little boy," he once said to one of his younger children, whose joyful glee at the approaching holidays he had gently checked,—"shall I tell you why I call it sad?" and he then repeated to him the simple story of his own early childhood,—how his own father had made him read to him a sermon on the text, "Boast not thyself of to-morrow," on the very Sunday evening before his sudden death. "Now cannot you see, when you talk with such certainty about this day week and what we shall do, why it seems sad to me?" But it was natural that such expressions should have been more often remarked by those who heard them during this year, even had they not been in themselves more frequent. "It is one of the most solemn things I do," he said to one of his children, who asked him why, in the titlepage of his MS. volume of sermons, he always wrote the date only of its commencement, and left a blank for that of its completion,—"to write the beginning of that sentence, and think that I may perhaps not live to finish it." And his pupils recollected the manner in which he had announced to them, before morning prayers, the unexpected death of one of their number: "We ought all to take to ourselves these repeated warnings; God, in his mercy, sends them to us. I say in his *mercy*, because they are warnings to all of us here,—we ought all to feel them as such,"—adding emphatically,—"and I am sure I feel it so myself."

Whatever might be the general interest of this

closing period, was deepened during the last month by accidental causes, into which it is not necessary to enter, but which became the means of drawing forth all the natural tenderness of his character more fully than any previous passage of his life. There was something in the added gentleness and kindness of his whole manner and conversation, — watching himself, and recalling his words if he thought they would be understood unkindly, — which even in his more general intercourse would make almost every one who saw him at that time connect their last recollections of him with some trait of thoughtfulness for others, and forgetfulness of himself, and which, to those nearest and dearest to him, seemed to awaken a consciousness, amounting almost to awe, of a visible growth in those qualities which are most naturally connected with the thought of another world. There was something also in the expressions of his own more personal feelings, — few and short as they ever were, but for that reason the more impressive when they did escape him, — which stamped them with a more than usual solemnity. Such were some of the passages in a private diary, which he now commenced for the first time, but not known till after his death by any, except her who alone shared his inmost thoughts, and who could not but treasure up in her memory every word connected with the beginning of this custom. It was about three weeks before his end, whilst confined to his room for a few days by an attack of feverish illness, to which, especially when in anxiety, he had always from time to time been liable, that he called her to his bedside, and expressed to her how, within the last few days, he seemed to have "felt quite a rush of love in his heart towards God and Christ;" and how he hoped that "all this might make him more gentle and tender," and that he might not soon lose the impression thus made upon him; adding, that, as a help to keeping it alive, he intended to write something in the evenings before he retired to rest.

From this diary, written the last thing at night, not daily, but from time to time in each week, it has been thought right to give the following extracts : —

"MAY 22. — I am now within a few weeks of completing my forty-seventh year. Am I not old enough to view life as it is, and to contemplate steadily its end — what it is coming to, and must come to — what all things are without God? I know that my senses are on the very eve of becoming weaker, and that my faculties, will then soon begin to decline too, — whether rapidly or not, I know not — but they will decline. Is there not one faculty which never declines, which is the seed and the seal of immortality? and what has become of that faculty in me? What is it to live unto God? May God open my eyes to see him by faith, in and through his Son Jesus Christ! may he draw me to him, and keep me with him, making his will my will, his love my love, his strength my strength! and may he make me feel that pretended strength, not derived from him, is no strength, but the worst weakness! May his strength be perfected in my weakness!

"TUESDAY EVENING, MAY 24. — Two days have passed, and I am mercifully restored to my health and strength. To-morrow I hope to be able to resume my usual duties. Now, then, is the dangerous moment. . . . O gracious Father! keep me now through thy Holy Spirit; keep my heart soft and tender now in health and amidst the bustle of the world; keep the thought of thyself present to me as my Father in Jesus Christ; and keep alive in me a spirit of love and meekness to all men, that I may be at once gentle and active and firm. Oh, strengthen me to bear pain or sickness or danger, or whatever thou shalt be pleased to lay upon me, as Christ's soldier and servant! and let my faith overcome the world daily. Strengthen my faith, that I may realize to my mind the things eternal, — death and things after death, and thyself. Oh, save me from my sins, from myself, and from my spiritual enemy, and keep me ever thine through Jesus Christ! Lord, hear my prayers also for my dearest wife, my dear children, my many and kind friends, my household, — for all those committed to my care, and for us to whom they are committed: I pray also for our country, and for thy holy Church in all the world. Perfect and bless the work of thy Spirit in the hearts of all thy people; and may thy kingdom come, and thy will be done in earth as it is in heaven! I pray for this, and for all that thou seest me to need, for Jesus Christ's sake.

"WEDNESDAY, MAY 25. — Again, before I go to rest, would I commit myself to God's care, through Christ, beseeching him to forgive me all my sins of this day past, and to keep alive his grace in my heart, and to cleanse me from all indolence, pride, harshness, and selfishness, and to give me the spirit of meekness, humility, firmness, and love. O Lord! keep thyself present to me ever, and perfect thy strength in my weakness. Take me and mine under thy blessed care, this night and evermore, through Jesus Christ.

"THURSDAY, MAY 26. . . . O Lord! keep thyself present to me always, and teach me to come to thee by the One and Living Way, thy Son Jesus Christ. Keep me humble and gentle. 2. Self-denying. 3. Firm and patient. 4. Active. 5. Wise to know thy will, and to discern the truth. 6. Loving, that I may learn to resemble thee and my Saviour. O Lord! forgive me for all my sins, and save me and guide me and strengthen me through Jesus Christ.

"MAY 29. . . . O Lord! save me from idle words, and grant that my heart may be truly cleansed and filled with thy Holy Spirit, and that I may arise to serve thee, and lie down to sleep in entire confidence in thee, and submission to thy will, ready for life or for death. Let me live for the day, not over-charged with worldly cares, but feeling that my treasure is not here, and desiring truly to be joined to thee in thy heavenly kingdom, and to those who are already gone to thee. O Lord! let me wait on patiently; but do thou save me from sin, and guide me with thy Spirit, and keep me with thee, and in faithful obedience to thee, through Jesus Christ thy Son our Lord.

"MAY 31. — Another day and another month succeed. May God keep my mind and heart fixed on him, and cleanse me from all sin! I would wish to keep a watch over my tongue, as to vehement speaking and censuring of others. I would desire to be more thoughtful of others, more thoughtful 'ultro' of my own head, without the suggestions of others. I would desire to remember my latter end, to which I am approaching, going down the hill of life, and having done far more than half my work. May God keep me in the hour of death, through Jesus Christ, and preserve me from over fear, as well as from presumption! Now, O Lord! whilst I am in health, keep my heart fixed on thee by faith, and then I shall not lose thee in sickness or in death. Guide and strengthen and enkindle me, and bless those dearest to me, and those committed to my charge, and keep them thine, and guide and support them in thy holy ways. Keep sin far from them, O Lord! and let it not come upon them through any neglect of mine. O Lord! inspire me with zeal, and guide me with wisdom, that thy name may be known to those committed to my care, and that they may be made and kept always thine. Grant this, O Lord! through Jesus Christ my Saviour, and may my whole trust towards thee be through his merits and intercessions!

"THURSDAY EVENING, JUNE 2. — Again the day is over, and I am going to rest. O Lord! preserve me this night, and strengthen me to bear whatever thou shalt see fit to lay on me, whether pain, sickness, danger, or distress.

"SUNDAY, JUNE 5.—I have been just looking over a newspaper, one of the most painful and solemn studies in the world if it be read thoughtfully. So much of sin and so much of suffering in the world, as are there displayed, and no one seems able to remedy either. And then the thought of my own private life, so full of comforts, is very startling when I contrast it with the lot of millions, whose portion is so full of distress or of trouble. May I be kept humble and zealous, and may God give me grace to labor in my generation for the good of my brethren, and for his glory! May he keep me his by night and by day, and strengthen me to bear and to do his will, through Jesus Christ!"

[LAST DAY, JUNE 11.]

On Saturday morning he was busily employed in examining some of the boys in Ranke's " History of the Popes," in the preparation of which he had sat up late on the previous night ; and some of the answers which had pleased him he recounted with great interest at breakfast. The chief part of the day he was engaged in finishing the business of the school, not accepting proffered assistance, even in the mechanical details, but going through the whole work himself. He went his usual round of the school to distribute the prizes to the boys before their final dispersion, and to take leave of those who were not returning after the holidays. "One more lesson," he had said to his own form on the previous evening, "I shall have with you on Sunday afternoon, and then I will say to you what I have to say." That parting address to which they were always accustomed to look forward with such pleasure, never came. But it is not to be wondered at, if they remarked with peculiar interest, that the last subject which he had set them for an exercise was " Domus Ultima ; " that the last translation for Latin verses was from the touching lines on the death of Sir Philip Sidney, in Spenser's " Ruins of Time ; " that the last words with which he closed his last lecture on the New Testament were in commenting on the passage of St. John, " It doth not yet appear what we shall be : but we know that, when he shall appear, we shall be like him ; for we shall see him as he is."— "So, too," he said, " in the Corinthians, ' For now we see through a glass darkly, but then face to face.' — Yes," he added, with marked fervency, "the mere contemplation of Christ shall transform us into his likeness."

In the afternoon he took his ordinary walk and bathe, enjoying the rare beauty of the day ; and he stopped again and again to look up into the unclouded blue of the summer sky, " the blue depth of ether " which had been at all times one of his most favorite images in nature, "conveying," as he said, " ideas so much more beautiful, as well as more true, than the ancient conceptions of the heavens as an iron firmament." At dinner he was in high spirits, talking with his several guests on subjects of social or historical interest, and recurring with great pleasure to his early geological studies, and describing with much interest his recent visit to Naseby with Carlyle, " its position on some of the highest table land in England, —the streams falling on the one side into the Atlantic, on the other into the German Ocean, — far away, too, from any town, — Market Harborough, the nearest, into which the Cavaliers were chased, late in the long summer evening, on the fourteenth of June, you know.''

In the evening he took a short stroll, as usual, on the lawn in the further garden, with the friend, and former pupil, from whom the account of these last conversations has been chiefly derived. His conversation with him turned on some points in the school of Oxford Theology, in regard to which he thought him to be in error : particularly he dwelt seriously, but kindly, on what he conceived to be false notions of the Eucharist, — insisting especially, that our Lord forbids us to suppose that the highest spiritual blessings can be conferred only or chiefly through the reception of material elements, — urging with great earnestness, when it was said that there might be various modes of spiritual agency, " My dear Lake, God be praised, we *are* told the great mode by which we are affected, — we have his own blessed assurance, ' The words which I speak unto you, they are spirit, and they are life.' ''

At nine o'clock was a supper, which, on the last evening of the summer half-year, he gave to the Sixth-Form boys of his own house ; and they were struck with the cheerfulness and liveliness of his manner, talking of the end of the half-year, and the pleasure of his return to Fox How in the next week, and observing, in allusion to the departure of so many of the boys, " How strange the chapel will look to-morrow ! "

The school business was now completely over. The old schoolhouse servant, who had been about the place many years, came to receive the final accounts, and delighted afterwards to tell how his master had kept him a quarter of an hour talking to him with more than usual kindness and confidence.

One more act, the last before he retired that night, remains to be recorded, — the last entry in his diary, which was not known or seen till the next morning, when it was discovered by those to whom every word bore a weight and meaning which he who wrote it had but little anticipated.

"SATURDAY EVENING, JUNE 11. — The day after to-morrow is my birthday, if I am permitted to live to see it, — my forty-seventh birthday since my birth. How large a portion of my life on earth is already passed! And then — what is to follow this life? How visibly my outward work seems contracting and softening away into the gentler employments of old age. In one sense, how nearly can I now say, ' Vixi.' And I thank God, that, as far as ambition is concerned, it is, I trust, fully mortified : I have no desire other than to step back from my present place in the world, and not to rise to a higher. Still, there are works, which, with God's permission, I would do before the night cometh, — especially that great work, if I might be permitted to take part in it. But above all, let me mind my own personal work, — to keep myself pure and zealous and believing, — laboring to do God's will, yet not anxious that it should be done by me rather than by others, if God disapproves of my doing it."

It was between five and six o'clock on Sunday morning that he awoke with a sharp pain across his chest, which he mentioned to his wife, on her asking whether he felt well, — adding that he had felt it slightly on the preceding day, before and after bathing. He then again composed himself to sleep : but her watchful care, always anxious, even to nervousness, at the least indication of illness, was at once awakened ; and on finding from him that the pain increased, and that it seemed to pass from his chest to his left arm, her alarm was so much aroused from a remembrance of having heard of this in connection with angina pectoris, and its fatal consequences, that, in spite of his remonstrances, she rose, and called up an old servant, whom they usually consulted in cases of illness, from her having so long attended the sick-bed of his sister Susannah. Re-assured by her confidence that there was no ground for fear, but still anxious, Mrs. Arnold returned to his room. She observed him, as she was dressing herself, lying still, but with his hands clasped, his lips moving, and his eyes raised upwards, as if engaged in prayer, when all at once he repeated, firmly and earnestly, " And Jesus said unto him, Thomas, because thou hast seen, thou hast believed : blessed are they who have not seen, and yet have believed ; " and soon afterwards, with a solemnity of manner and depth of utterance which spoke more than the words themselves, " But if ye be without chastisement, whereof all are partakers, then are ye bastards, and not sons."

From time to time he seemed to be in severe suffering, and, on the entrance of the old servant before mentioned, said, " Ah, Elizabeth ! if I had been as

much accustomed to pain as dear Susannah was, I
should bear it better." To his wife, however, he
uttered no expressions of acute pain, dwelling only on
the moments of comparative ease, and observing that
he did not know what it was. But the more than
usual earnestness which marked his tone and manner,
especially in repeating the verses from Scripture, had
again aroused her worst fears ; and she ordered mes-
sengers to be sent for medical assistance, which he
had at first requested her not to do, from not liking to
disturb at that early hour the usual medical attendant,
who had been suffering from indisposition. She then
took up the Prayer Book, and was looking for a Psalm
to read to him, when he said quickly, " The fifty-first,"
— which she accordingly read by his bedside, remind-
ing him, at the seventh verse, that it was the favorite
verse of one of the old almswomen whom he was in
the habit of visiting ; and at the twelfth verse, " O give
me the comfort of thy help again, and stablish me
with thy free Spirit : " he repeated it after her very
earnestly. She then read the prayer in the " Visitation
of the Sick," beginning, " The Almighty Lord, who is
a most strong tower," etc., kneeling herself at the foot
of the bed, and altering it into a common prayer for
them both.

As the clock struck a quarter to seven, Dr. Bucknill
(the son of the usual medical attendant) entered the
room. He was then lying on his back, his countenance much as usual ; his pulse, though regular, was
very quick ; and there was cold perspiration on the brow

and cheeks. But his tone was cheerful. "How is your father?" he asked, on the physician's entrance: "I am sorry to disturb you so early: I knew that your father was unwell, and that you had enough to do." He described the pain, speaking of it as having been very severe, and then said, "What is it?" Whilst the physician was pausing for a moment before he replied, the pain returned, and remedies were applied till it passed away; and Mrs. Arnold, seeing by the measures used that the medical man was himself alarmed, left the room for a few moments to call up her second son, the eldest of the family then at Rugby, and impart her anxiety to him; and during her absence her husband again asked what it was, and was answered that it was spasm of the heart. He exclaimed, in his peculiar manner of recognition, "Ha!" and then, on being asked if he had ever in his life fainted, "No, never." If he had ever had difficulty of breathing? "No, never." If he had ever had sharp pain in the chest? "No, never." If any of his family had ever had disease of the chest? "Yes, my father had — he died of it." — "What age was he?" — "Fifty-three." — "Was it suddenly fatal?" — "Yes, suddenly fatal." He then asked if disease of the heart was a common disease? "Not very common." — "Where do we find it most?" — "In large towns, I think." — "Why?" (Two or three causes were mentioned.) "Is it generally fatal?" — "Yes, I am afraid it is."

The physician then quitted the house for medicine, leaving Mrs. Arnold, now fully aware from him of her

husband's state. At this moment she was joined by
her son, who entered the room with no serious apprehension ; and, on his coming up to the bed, his father,
with his usual gladness of expression towards him,
asked, "How is your deafness, my boy?" (he had
been suffering from it the night before) ; and then,
playfully alluding to an old accusation against him,
"You must not stay here : you know you do not like a
sick-room." He then sat down with his mother at the
foot of the bed ; and presently his father said in a low
voice, "My son, thank God for me !" and, as his son
did not at once catch his meaning, he went on, saying,
"Thank God, Tom, for giving me this pain. I have
suffered so little pain in my life, that I feel it is very
good for me : now God has given it to me, and I do
so thank him for it." And again, after a pause, he
said, — alluding to a wish which his son had often
heard him express, that, if he ever had to suffer pain,
his faculties might be unaffected by it, — "How thankful I am that my head is untouched." Meanwhile his
wife, who still had sounding in her ears the tone in
which he had repeated the passage from the Epistle to
the Hebrews, again turned to the Prayer Book, and
began to read the Exhortation in which it occurs in
the "Visitation of the Sick." He listened with deep
attention, saying emphatically, "Yes," at the end of
many of the sentences. "There should be no greater
comfort to Christian persons than to be made like unto
Christ." — "Yes." — "By suffering patiently troubles,
adversities, and sickness." — "Yes." — "He entered

not into his glory before he was crucified."—"Yes."
At the words, "everlasting life," she stopped; and his
son said, "I wish, dear papa, we had you at Fox
How." He made no answer; but the last conscious
look, which remained fixed in his wife's memory, was
the look of intense tenderness and love with which he
smiled upon them both at that moment.

The physician now returned with the medicines,
and the former remedies were applied: there was a
slight return of the spasms, after which he said, "If
the pain is again as severe as it was before you came,
I do not know how I can bear it." He then, with
his eyes fixed upon the physician, who rather felt than
saw them upon him, so as to make it impossible not
to answer the exact truth, repeated one or two of his
former questions about the cause of the disease, and
ended with asking, "Is it likely to return?" and, on
being told that it was, "Is it generally suddenly fatal?"
—"Generally." On being asked whether he had any
pain, he replied that he had none, but from the mus-
tard plaster on his chest, with a remark on the severity
of the spasms in comparison with this outward pain,
and then, a few moments afterwards, inquired what
medicine was to be given, and on being told, answered,
"Ah! very well." The physician, who was dropping
the laudanum into a glass, turned round, and saw him
looking quite calm, but with his eyes shut. In another
minute he heard a rattle in the throat, and a convulsive
struggle, — flew to the bed, caught his head upon his
shoulder, and called to one of the servants to fetch

Mrs. Arnold. She had but just left the room before his last conversation with the physician, in order to acquaint her son with his father's danger, of which he was still unconscious, when she heard herself called from above. She rushed up-stairs, told her son to bring the rest of the children, and with her own hands applied the remedies that were brought, in the hope of reviving animation, though herself feeling, from the moment that she saw him, that he had already passed away. He was indeed no longer conscious. The sobs and cries of his children, as they entered and saw their father's state, made no impression upon him : the eyes were fixed ; the countenance was unmoved ; there was a heaving of the chest ; deep gasps escaped at prolonged intervals ; and just as the usual medical attendant arrived, and as the old schoolhouse servant, in an agony of grief, rushed with the others into the room, in the hope of seeing his master once more, he breathed his last.

It must have been shortly before eight A.M. that he expired, though it was naturally impossible for those who were present to adjust their recollections of what passed with precise exactness of time or place. So short and sudden had been the seizure, that hardly any one out of the household itself had heard of his illness before its fatal close. His guest, and former pupil (who had slept in a remote part of the house), was coming down to breakfast as usual, thinking of questions to which the conversation of the preceding night had given rise, and which, by the great kindness of his manner, he felt doubly encouraged to ask him, when he was met on the staircase by the announcement of his death. The masters knew nothing till the moment when, almost at the same time at the different boarding-houses, the fatal message was delivered in all its startling abruptness, " that Dr. Arnold was dead." What that Sunday was in Rugby it is hard fully to represent, — the incredulity, the bewilderment, the agitating inquiries for every detail ; the blank, more awful than sorrow, that prevailed through the vacant services of that long and dreary day ; the feeling as if the very place had passed away with him who had so emphatically been in every sense its head ; the sympathy which hardly dared to contemplate, and which yet could not but fix the thoughts and looks of all on the desolate house, where the fatherless family were gathered round the chamber of death.

Five of his children were awaiting their father's arrival at Fox How. To them the news was brought on Monday morning, by the same pupil who had been in the house at his death, and who long would remember the hour when he reached the place, just as the early summer dawn — the dawn of that forty-seventh birthday — was breaking over that beautiful valley, every shrub and every flower in all its freshness and luxuriance, speaking of him who had so tenderly fostered their growth around the destined home of his old age. On the evening of that day, which they had been fondly preparing to celebrate with its usual pleasures, they arrived at Rugby in time to see their father's face in death.

He was buried on the following Friday, the very day week, since, from the same house, two and two in like manner, so many of those who now joined in the funeral procession to the chapel, had followed him in full health and vigor to the public speeches in the school. It was attended by his whole family, by those of his friends and former pupils who had assembled from various parts during the week, and by many of the neighboring clergy and of the inhabitants of the town, both rich and poor. The ceremony was performed by Mr. Moultrie, rector of Rugby, from that place which, for fourteen years, had been occupied only by him who was gone, and to whom every part of that chapel owed its peculiar interest ; and his remains were deposited in the chancel immediately under the communion-table.

Once more his family met in the chapel on the following Sunday, and partook of the holy communion at his grave, and heard read the sermon preached by him in the preceding year, on " Faith Triumphant in Death."   And yet one more service in connection with him took place in the chapel, when, on the first Sunday of the next half-year, the school, which had dispersed on the eve of his death, assembled again within its walls under his successor, and witnessed in the funeral services with which that day was observed, the last public tribute of sorrow to their departed master.

www.ingramcontent.com/pod-product-compliance
Lightning Source LLC
Chambersburg PA
CBHW031421020726
47499CB00005B/1533